SAVAGE HER REPLY

DEIRDRE SULLIVAN

ILLUSTRATED BY KAREN VAUGHAN

Little Island
Books create waves

A chairde,

The Children of Lir is one of Ireland's most popular legends. It exists in a strange liminal space — between paganism and Christianity, myth and fairytale.

It's a story of a woman who marries her sister's widower, who grows to resent his children, who turns them into swans. When this is discovered she is punished, but the spell cannot be reversed. The children live as swans until long after the world they grew up in is reshaped, until the Old Gods are replaced, until … well, I won't spoil it.

I don't remember the first time I heard the Children of Lir, but I remember being drawn to Aífe, the stepmother character, and fascinated by her power and the punishment she's forced to choose. What pushed her to react the way she did? How would she tell the story, if she had the space, the time, the words?

We tell stories to make sense of the world and each other, to foster connection and understanding. In telling this story, I am connected to all who told it before me, all who will tell it after, and of course, to everyone who reads it. That's a powerful thing, and one I don't take lightly.

Go raibh maith agaibh,

Deirdre Sullivan,

2023

At the end of this book you will find a guide to some of the Irish names and words used in the story.

Scan here to see a short video of Deirdre reading from the book

SAVAGE HER REPLY
First published in 2020 by
Little Island Books
7 Kenilworth Park
Dublin 6w
Ireland

First published in the USA by Little Island in 2023

A British Library Cataloguing in Publication record for this book is available from
the British Library.

Cover and interior illustrations by Karen Vaughan
Typeset by Niall McCormack
Proofread by Emma Dunne
Printed in Poland by Skleniarz

Print ISBN: 978-1-912417-67-4
Ebook (Kindle) ISBN: 978-1-912417-65-0
Ebook (other platforms) ISBN: 978-1-912417-66-7

Little Island has received funding to support this book from
the Arts Council of Ireland

10 9 8 7 6 5 4 3 2

For Siobhán Parkinson

Le míle buíochas

'Savage her reply,' said Conare.
'Let her in, then, despite the geiss against it.'

From *Early Irish Myths and Sagas*
(Jeffrey Gantz, 1981)

NUIN

stories vary, throat to throat, and heart to foolish heart

but mine belongs to me

as much as them

so here I am

I will begin again

I will remember

I am old. I am older than books, I am older than keep cups, I am older than the internet, I am older than Christ, I am older than trains. I am older than your oldest living relative's oldest memory and her mother's before her and *her* mother's before *her* and you could keep on going, going, going. I am older than your governments, your laws, I am older than bus stops, I am older than the words you shape inside your mouth and I am older than your mouth. The tongue I spoke when I was something else has changed entirely and it sounds jarring in this bright and humming world. I am older than electricity, I am older than oil lamps, I am older than the alphabet, I am older than the months you use, I am older than chocolate, I am older than Christmas, I am older than iron.

And yet ... I am younger than blood, than salt, than sea. I am younger than war, I am younger than heroes, I am younger than marriage, I am younger than Tara, I am younger than tears, I am younger than poetry, I am younger than time, I am younger than cats, I am younger than wolves, I am younger than swans, I am younger than stones, I am younger than the Boyne, I am younger than people wanting things they cannot have, I am younger than thirst, I am younger than bread, I am younger than spells, I am younger than trees, I am younger than knives, I am younger than hands, I am younger than sleep, I am younger than sex, I am younger than breath, I am younger than rage, I am younger than bones, I am younger than the lake that welcomed their despair, I am younger than birth, I am younger than death, I am younger than hate, I am younger than love, I am younger than hope, I am younger than Ireland, I am younger than horses, I am younger than a child's despair, I am younger than pleading, I am younger than cruelty, I am younger than earrings, I am younger than mercy, I am younger than sorcery, I am younger than kisses, I am younger than boats, I am younger than storms, I am younger than feathers, I am younger than thrones, I am younger than fathers, I am younger than husbands, I am younger than answers.

I am younger than milk.

And when you read about the things I did, the thing that I've become, try your best to reach out and to meet me.

Here.

Before all this.

I was a little girl.

And someone took me.

NGETAL

so many   things that

used to speak and   scream

now   are silent

I must explain what's left of me to someone

SCÉAL

*Long, long ago in Ireland, the time came to elect a new high king. The
chieftains from all five provinces assembled, and it was decided that
Bodhbh Dearg, or Bodhbh the Red, was the man for the job, which left
Lir of Sídh Finnachadh in a fury. He left that place in dark humour,
and returned home to more misfortune. His dear wife became ill and
died soon after. The new high king, in his wisdom, generously offered
Lir the hand of one of his three foster-daughters to replace the woman
that he had lost. Lir chose the eldest and noblest, Aébh, and soon she
was with child, and they were happy.*

OIR

there were three of us ... and then there were two of us

Áebh, Aife

Ailbhe

once upon a time

we had each other

Some say destiny is woven by the skillful fingers of a goddess. Others claim that it is carved in stone. I don't remember my mother's hands, or how she used them. Our attendants were, in some way, mothers to us. They gave me much. But the relationship is different, I think. They were warrior women, sworn to keep us safe. I don't remember what my father looked like, what made him smile. It has been said to me that I was like him. Comments made in passing, but I held to them like jewels. We missed our family, but we understood why we had to leave. Bodhbh had asked for us, and our parents wanted what they had to be safe. They needed his protection, power, kinship. And so they gave us up. It wasn't supposed to be for ever. We were supposed to return more connected, not less. We were supposed to return.

There are them that think we forge our own destiny. After all this time, I am still unsure. Apart from this: I know that I don't know. That there are things we do and do not choose. We are ourselves, and we are also stories people tell. When we faded from our parents' lives, we must have become a different sort of thing to what we were. An honour or a threat. Or something blurry in between the two. It cannot have been easy to let us go, their only children, Ailbhe just a babe. With fosterings it was unusual to take all that a person had. But our foster-father was an unusual sort of man, and it was necessary to indulge him. People can always find ways to twist customs and traditions to suit their own ends. Those who love power will gather power. And it will never be as warm and trusting as the skin of a sleeping child, but that sort of thing is hard to value when your eyes are fixed upon a crown.

My sisters and I crossed the sea on a tiny boat that smelt of wood and leather and the sea-spray kissed our little faces. The three of us together, as it always was, from there on out. Aébh, the eldest, and Ailbhe, the baby. And myself, in the middle. We huddled together like kittens in the bottom of the vessel, watching the sure hands and grim faces of the women who attended us. And it was frightening, and it was cold. I know that there are siblings who do not love each other as we did. Had we been left at home, perhaps we would have drifted apart. We were different sorts of people the one from the other, but all of us clung to this half-remembered dream of home. We fed each other with it. Where we were going, this was beyond price.

I was very good, the women said. I only roared when they put me on land. As though I could feel myself being pulled from where I'd been, from who I was and all I could become. A roar, they said. They wanted us to be like them, like warriors. Strong and sure, adapting seamlessly to all that was required. And I just wanted somewhere to belong. I craved a sense of ownership over my home, my clothes, my words, my heart, my body. I can't have been an easy child to guard, and Dechtaire and Smól must have been very glad of my sisters at times, that they distracted me from my screamings and my rantings at the various slights and denials that were always being visited upon me. I often, as a child, imagined an invisible hand reaching from the place that hurts the most when you've been running, that little stitch that throbs beneath the heart, over the fields and hills towards the stones and mountains, to where the sea fights earth and over that again. And to what?

To faces I don't know, that wouldn't know me.

The stars were bright that night, as the boat moved through the water, and we could see them. When we arrived at the shore, there were chariots and horses waiting. Dechtaire and Smól bundled our stuff on to them and continued towards Sídh Femuin, the home of Bodhbh the Red. I remember so little of what happened to me before then. Of the place I came from. But that journey that began my transition from daughter to fosterling is a vivid one. The cold wind and the wild sea and the bright stars. The grass was grey, and after a time, everything faded from my vision till the morning. But I kept those stars inside me, wondering if I could read them, know them, and would what lay ahead be as terrifying as that first departure. Would I always long for the sound of my father, the smell of my mother, the warmth of my hearth? Was there any comfort to be had? I couldn't find much. Later on, I learned to look at the stars a little differently. And now they are old friends, though it is rarely that I try to read them. The future stretches wide and is hard to look at. The past is not so easy, mind you, either.

DUIR

oak trees grow from acorns

and tales

from mouths

Our people were different in many ways to the humans of today, longer limbed and longer lived, but there were similarities as well. Perhaps that is why so many of our stories still survive. The overlapping pieces of our hearts. I was young in the time before things were written down. Druids memorised our history and lore, fed it back to us, and gained importance. People heard things and told them to other people, to lengthen evenings or to shorten roads. But, even with events that really happened, with every teller something tends to change. Hair colour, or the food served at a feast. The number of eyes in your head, the number of scars on your back. The right and wrong of it. We put ourselves into the tales we tell, and to do that, we must remove a part of someone else.

Stories can be weapons, persuading people of things about themselves, about each other. Before I was in one, I loved to listen. To gather things around me, bits of knowledge. I would seek out druids, poets, musicians, gossips, warriors, and plague them with questions, until I was told that was enough. I would repeat the stories to my sisters and put extra pieces in to make them smile. A fight for Ailbhe, something sweet for Aébh. I loved them, so I looked to make them happy. They were all I had now, in this place. And wasn't I lucky to have them by my side, as I grew up in the home of Bodhbh the Red, where loyalty was as valuable as its uses, and we were a hold he had on someone else.

Our foster-father was a strange and charismatic sort of man. In those days, there were smaller kings and then a high king to unite them. When we encountered him first, he had yet to be elected high king, but had established a powerful reputation. His place was large and comfortable, and his allies plentiful. Many fine fat cows grazed on his lands, and powerful bulls as well. As a ruler, he was famous for his wisdom and ability to solve problems to the satisfaction, largely, of all concerned. Kingship pleased him, and his people pleased him. We tried our best to please him in a different way, out of desperation or a need for love. If he had asked one of us for a hand, we would have cut it off for him without a moment's thought. Our family needed him. We needed him. And he could be kind. He exuded warmth and fairness. People liked him. He was ambitious, for himself as well as for his people. A better king than most.

But always busy. We would gather around him sometimes and he would ruffle our hair and ask us how we were getting on, study our strengths, our faces and our forms. I thought back then he cared, that it was interest, not assessment.

His wife, Ban, was a kind woman, but distant. She had her own children, and a household to run, and we were fed and clothed and taught skills that would help us to be useful to Bodhbh as we aged. Managing a *sidh*, bartering, presenting ourselves well, repairing clothes, arranging hair, speaking softly, listening well. Making sure we knew who people were and their place and function in relation to our own. Being a credit to our foster-father. Everything on the territory he ruled over, his *tuath*, reflected him and on him. We were a sacrifice at his altar. The jewels upon his fingers, round his neck.

Let me draw you a picture of him, as I remember. It was said of him that he was the son of our great god, the Dagda, and in his presence you could well believe it. His voice was deep and resonant, and he had a booming laugh that made all who heard it laugh along. People didn't seem to try to curry favour for favour's sake with Bodhbh. They wanted him to like them, because he was a marvellous sort of man, and his good opinion could help a person on the inside as well as on the outside. He didn't need to taste a magic fish to give him wisdom. Years of experience, combined with his powerful lineage, had given him solidity and the appearance of trustworthiness. There was a weight to him, like a well-made sword. He had a ruddy face, a two-forked beard. Long golden hair that tumbled past his shoulders. He generally wore it held back with either a leather thong or a thin gold thread. Skin like hide. His hands were large and inelegant, with wide palms and long, thick fingers. They were always doing something, or about to do something. A vow. A threat.

Bodhbh's features underneath the beard were delicate, almost feminine. His body tall and broad, his arms thick. He could wrap his hands around your ribcage and throw you up in the air, and the fear and delight would consume you.

We were rarely, if ever, alone with him. He had nine warriors he kept around him. And they were nice men too, but fierce. We used to try to get them to smile at us, and sometimes one of them would and we would laugh, triumphant, at each other. A strange game, but satisfying too. Aébh, being lovely, was the best at that, as easy to like as I was hard to take.

Bodhbh's feet were big, and his smallest toes tilted to the side so that the nail pointed out towards the walls, rather than up towards the roof. Sometimes he would have hairs in his nose or ears and sometimes they would be gone. I never knew what he did with them.

He was kind. He was. He did his duty by us and more besides. But we were an investment. Calves in a field. A lush field, full of clover. Sun in the sky and milk inside our bellies. Of course we hoped, of course we played together. And didn't think that we would become cows and then meat to be served to this warrior or that one, until there was nothing left of us but memory.

There was a little lip of stone behind the raised part of the central room of the *sídh,* where Bodhbh sat deciding things for people, or watching them eat and move with his bright gull's eyes. When I was a girl, I could squeeze behind that lip and listen to everything that was said. There were other places too, underneath cloaks, beneath tables or behind wall-hangings. The larger I grew the more difficult it was, but I enjoyed a challenge. I became adept at reading shadows on the wall. There was a sense of anticipation and power when I was listening, unseen, to conversations others were not privy to. I was fascinated by private things and always curious to find out more about our parents, how they fared on the rough and beautiful island they called home. I rarely heard their names, as they were not as powerful as he, and their loyalty was secure as long as he possessed the three of us.

I remember the first time he caught me. Our eyes met and his mouth crooked with amusement, and he let me stay tucked behind that thick lip of stone, my heart racing, until everyone had left. And then he pulled me out with his big hands and brushed my hair from my face. I was so frightened, I burst in to tears, but he told me what a brave, bold girl I was. How useful sharp ears were to him at times. He asked me if I would let him know the things I heard when no-one knew I was there. Especially if the man Lir was mentioned.

That was the first time I heard that name.

COLL

it's hard to know how to protect yourself

from

those

you

love

Our attendants, Dechtaire and Smól, were warrior women, tall and strong, and Ailbhe adored the pair of them. The same way I would follow druids around, she followed them. But when she asked them questions, they gave answers. Sometimes curtly, but always with a kindness underneath.

They loved each other. When we were alone, they would always be touching. Fingers interlacing, hands kneading at shoulders. They taught me, all of us, to fight, from when we were very young. And though it never became second nature to me the way it did to Ailbhe, I wasn't bad. I loved to get a slight nod of the head. A 'well done'. They would tell me stories about power and the different ways it looked. About battlefield goddesses and great queens. And I would be repeating what they told me back to myself in my head so I could share it with others. Trying to get it right.

When I was nine, a visiting chieftain tried to put his hands on me and I broke three of his fingers. He came to them, complaining, and had to be carried from the room on a litter. We laughed at that. I felt protected by them. We all did. They were from home, and though neither my sisters nor myself could remember much about the place we came from, our father Oillill of Aran and our mother Éabha, Dechtaire and Smól could and did provide us with snippets, so often sought and shared that they became as vivid as memories, and certainly as valued. Our father quiet, more poet than king. His wife, our mother, talkative, and charming. Both well able to handle themselves in battle. My face was like his face, my hair like hers. Aébh had her smooth way of moving, and Ailbhe had her talent with a spear. Our parents had an affinity for water, and we shared that. But it was normal then. Magic flowed through the world more forcefully, and freely, and if you had a mind to reach your fingers out, you could train yourself to touch it, use it.

Our people were the Tuatha Dé Danann, the children of the goddess Danu, she of the sacred waters. And though the king was generally a man, sovereignty itself was feminine, mysterious. The land had to welcome the king. To want him to rule. Home was an agreement then, between the land and the people living on it. It wasn't a matter of deciding something was your own and taking it, there had to be a thing that recognised you. And whether that was because you were wise and brave and powerful and all the traditional qualities we tell ourselves kings have, or because it liked the taste of blood, well, time would tell. The earth can be an angry thing as well. Can strike out at the lives that live upon it. And our lives were long, if we survived the different ways we hurt each other. Children were important to our people, and we had difficulty sometimes in the having and the keeping of them. To separate a parent from a child was no small thing.

The island we were born on still exists. I visit it sometimes, fly over the harsh rock and soft grass. I see the lash of water. How hard the people on it must have worked, how different a life would have been mine. And could I have been pleased with that? Would that small hand have rested or reached out across the ocean to something else entirely?

I was never satisfied with what I had.

I wanted more.

I wanted to be heard and to be loved.

I wanted to be favoured.

And I wasn't.

All my life I have been second best.

Dechtaire and Smól were for each other above all. Bodhbh was for himself. My sisters loved me well enough, I suppose, but we could not remain together always, not after Lir.

Lir was hard to read.

But certainly, he was never mine. Not wholly.

A child's want in a woman's heart is dangerous.

But I have jumped ahead. I will return. To where I need to be. I think that I have been silent too long, swooping here and there, meeting no-one. My thoughts are scattered, not strung together.

Time passed, my legs got longer and my back straighter, my small teeth were replaced by bigger teeth. I learned to be silent, more invisible. Absorbing everything, to share with my sisters, and sometimes, if I thought it worth his while, with Bodhbh. *Father* was what we wanted him to be, and what we called him, but the taste of that inside my mouth changed somewhat over time. I had grown worshipful of him. Dying for his notice, his approval. That curt nod of the head that meant, *This is useful, leave me.*

When knowledge mattered he went straight to work.

We, the Tuatha Dé Danann, were at war then. The Invaders had come from across the waves, and they would not return there, though we did our best to send them back. Perhaps we had neglected to honour the land as deeply as we should have, the druids more concerned with power and influence, though perhaps not that. Maybe there's a time for everything and this was theirs. There's destiny again. The land, it seemed, was choosing something else, another people. Time and again we tried to push them back. I say we, because that is what it felt like then. We, as a people, as one, child to adult, trying to hold fast to what we had. And it was terrifying. Things that had been certain were not certain. Who were these invaders who could calm down storms? Who stood against us, time and time again, and did not fall. We were not used to it. We did not like it.

Wisdom is just things that people know. And all we had known was crumbling into something else entirely, and the shape of our lives was about to change, just as our bodies were changing and growing. We didn't look like children any more. And there was a power and a threat in that. In the approach of adulthood.

Dechtaire and Smól left us and went to fight. On Bodhbh's orders and their own desire. Their faces flushed, they polished their weapons. Ailbhe stared at them, wild with the want to follow them. To have her own fine swords and spears and knives and battle garments. And Aébh's worry mirrored mine. They were strong and brave. They would fight well. They would protect each other. But there were other forces at work here, and I think we shared the sense that victory, if it came, would not be easy.

It wasn't easy. And it didn't come.

We spent months straining for pieces of news, hoping that the women who had reared us would survive unscathed. Ailbhe loved the notion of dying in battle. The glory of it. But all I could think of were cuts of meat. People into flesh. Into something to pull and tear apart. To be consumed by crows. I did not want that for Dechtaire and Smól. I wanted a future where they would be safe. There were many futures that I wanted, and the one I got would be the very last I would have picked.

A battle, at Tailtiú, sent them to the Otherworld. We received the news from one of Bodhbh's men, and I remember telling myself they were just attendants, not my parents. That I should not care so much. That really, when I thought on it, it was time for them to be gone from us, and we on the verge of womanhood, ready to grasp what came with both hands. Some of this spilled out of me as we grieved, and Ailbhe slapped me hard across the face. Aébh just looked at me and said my name. Softly and like this:

'Oh.

Aífe.'

She had a way of knowing, my eldest sister, the meat of what was in a person's heart, without them telling her in words. She listened closely. But in a different way to me, that was not a shield or a spear, but an embrace. She cared because she cared. The best of us. And I remember promising myself, and my sisters, that we would all meet again when it came our turn to cross over. That it would be as though no time had passed. And we would all be there, and close together. Aébh and Ailbhe beside me in the night, as we keened grief into the skins we slept on.

I had my sisters then. What wealth that was!

Our guardians were far from the only people to perish at Tailtiú. It was a time of fear and confusion. Bodhbh, who had waited like a cat looking at a pigeon for so long, finally wiggled his arse and pounced right at the kingship. He was elected high king, to great fanfare. His wisdom, his calm demeanour, his warmth and diplomacy made our people feel more confident, and we took pride in this. In the great man our foster-father was.

But not everyone was pleased with the decision. Many had supported Lir of Sídh Finnachadh, not least Lir himself. His expression neutral as he turned his heel and left the assembly, riding off without a single word. I followed him in the shadows, noticing the twist of his brow and the impatience with which he attended to his horses. The hard set of his mouth. He was, I observed, not a patient man.

When the Invaders were in their boats, nine waves away from shore, the druids summoned a terrifying storm to make them leave. Their poet asked the land to help and she obeyed him. Tranquillity can be a sort of threat.

After the assembly many of the men with Bodhbh took umbrage. Urged him to follow swiftly and with force. My foster-father did not frown or smile, but stroked the two forks of his golden beard, the one after the other.

Bodhbh asked me about Lir, afterwards. What my keen eyes had seen. And I told him, not knowing what the telling him would mean. He nodded, his mouth a straight line in the centre of the forest of his beard. The furrows in his brow were different to those in Smól's, I noticed. Hers were diagonal. His a straight, deep slash. I left him thinking how to handle this. It was a delicate matter, and later, when I had time and space to think on it, I realised how little I knew of its complexity.

We were a people at war. And it was important to present a united front. To find a way to keep ourselves together.

A creative person can always use their wits to find a way.

And very soon, poor Lir lost his wife, which gave my foster-father a fine new chance to exercise the wisdom and magnanimity that had earned him the kingship.

IDHO

but not your heart your heart will never stop it will keep hurting and it will keep beating

they will	come and
take the	things you need
to keep you safe and	tethered to the world
oh, it will stop	your breath
and stop	your mouth

There is a story of another Aífe. I used to like to hear it, as a child. This Aífe was a beauty, unlike me, and more than that, she was a merry soul. She loved to laugh. She took a lover, and his name was Iollan. Another woman also loved that man. And that woman, Ilbrach, looked at what Aífe had and she herself did not, and hate grew in her, so she made a plan. With smiles, she convinced Aífe to come swimming with her. When Ilbrach got her rival in the water, she took a wand and waved it in the air. She called the gods and land and railed against poor Aífe. She turned her from woman into crane. For two hundred years, until her death, Aífe lived with soft white feathers, long impressive legs and rounded wings. Her sad call filtering across the wetlands. But all was not lost, not fully, though it was a lonely life, and different. For Aífe's lover had been the son of Manannán Mac Lir, the sea god, for whom the sea was a welcoming, nourishing place, a lush meadow, speckled with purple flowers. As the curse drove Aífe from lake to lonely lake, he reached out with his power through her turmoil and did what he could to give the poor crane peace. He, perhaps in loyalty to useless, handsome Iollan, of whom we hear no more in this story, took her under his protection. But the protection of a powerful person can be a sort of horror in itself. As well I know.

They became close, and in some tellings he is called her husband. That detail isn't fixed, but one thing is: when eventually Aífe died, Manannán got his knife and flayed her corpse. Her skin he turned into the treasure bag of the Tuatha Dé Danann. And this, when people tell it, was an honour. I always wondered if she could pass easily into the Otherworld so mutilated. If it felt like an honour, when she knew. When she saw what had been done to her, after all that had been done already. Men kept their treasures in her skin for centuries, Lugh Lámhfhada and Fionn Mac Cumhaill among them.

The stories that we hear when we are children shape us, don't they? Some more than most. I hope that Ilbrach got to have her lover. I hope that it was worth it in the end. I leave it with more questions than I enter. I worry for the both of them.

And I wonder.

What she did. Was it worse or better than what I did?

What does it mean that no-one knows what happened to her next?

What did they do with what remained of Aífe? The bloody remnants of a noble creature. Did they bury her with proper honour? There is not a soul left in the world who will take the care to bury me in the style that sends me to my people when I go. They wouldn't even know what words to say.

Everyone who knew me back then is dead.

Two hundred years seemed such a long time when I was a girl, and now it's just a busy flash. I have lived so long that years are days. And things have changed, but some things haven't changed. Marriage then could be like marriage now. Love did exist, as did its companion, yearning. Divorce was easier. It had to be. We lived long lives, my people. Not always though. We felt death sharply when it came for one of our own, in battle or out of it. And, at this time, more and more of us were learning what loss did to you. What it was like to lose someone you loved. The hungry sort of hurt it left behind.

My sisters and I, in our grief, were not really prepared for what was coming. But we had been trained to obey and so we did. It became apparent that one of us was to be matched with Lir, to keep him loyal to Bodbh. It did make sense. We were now of child-bearing age, and Lir was the finest warrior we had, at a time of war. A great chieftain with a *sídh* famed for its beauty. His wife would have a comfortable life, and power. Status. She would be respected, even feared. His beard was greying even then and we were in the flower of our youth. That didn't matter, save that it would please him. He was an important man, and liked his women fresh.

Aébh was the eldest of us, though not by much, wide-hipped and pleasing of form. Flawless skin, dark eyes, a slender neck, just a shade too long. She accepted people as they were, while I interrogated what they could be. She was generally of a gentler disposition than I was. She almost never threw things, raised her voice. It was inevitable that Lir would choose her. She also wanted to be chosen. To be a wife, a mother. To have her own *sidh*. I often thought of a swan when I saw her in the company of others. The sleek, smooth way she moved and interacted. People liked to look at Aébh. But swans work hard. Underneath the surface of the water, their legs work fiercely and, if needs be, they can be as warlike as geese. They'll fight to keep their patch, or to protect their young.

Lir looked at Ailbhe, stocky and defiant in clothing that confined her. Her bare arms were covered in bruises, and her eyebrows fierce. She was short, a quality our people did not prize, and came up to the bottom of his chest. But every inch was muscle, and hard earned at that. Her beauty was not the sort a king appreciates.

He moved on, and looked me up and down. My breasts, my face. I was wearing green, my hair was flowing down my back, and there were thick gold ropes around my wrists and neck. I was the daughter of a king and the foster-daughter of a high king. And I put every bit of pride I had into meeting his eyes. And something passed between us, a sense of recognition.

And revulsion. I felt an eel coil within my stomach, pulsing in me. Weighing me down. Lir reached out his fingers, thick with rings, and tucked a strand of hair behind my ear. His breath upon my neck and I was frightened. He was gentle. Lir was always gentle. But still, he let me know. Who he was and that I could be had.

And that he didn't want me. A little click of tongue against his teeth, and Lir moved on.

And once he noticed Aébh, her fate was sealed. But as I looked at her, her face was flushed, her eyes bright. She looked over at our foster-father smiling. And Lir smiled too, and Bodhbh. He took her hand and said she was the fairest, noblest one and would be his. Sometimes destiny is no great hardship.

They were wed that night, and the next morning, my sister was gone, to live in Sídh Finnachadh. She embraced me before she left, and I watched the two of them, their chariot flanked by nine warriors, their backs straight and their cloaks bright. Two proud swans, swimming towards the future. Away from me.

And I felt sick.

Some of it relief.

I didn't want him.

Some of it was fear.

But a good portion of it was shame.

And jealousy, perhaps. I loved my sister deeply. Ailbhe I adored, but there was a self-sufficiency about her, a ferocity. I had the sense that one day we would wake and she would just be gone. Become a warrior outside the tribe, accomplishing feats myself and Aébh would hear about in songs. And it would take some time to get to that, it would. But it was coming. I could see it in the air murmuring through the leaves, the run of the water and the slop of blood. I had been asking questions of the old ones. I had the good sense, even then, to fear for the future.

I would be more alone without my Aébh. And at the same time, her new life, the future that she wanted, had begun. She would be a good wife, would have babies. And she had been held above myself and Ailbhe. Before my king, our foster-father, and his retinue. The whole *tuath* would surely know by now.

How much better she was than both of us.

And there was a sting to that they would enjoy.

SCÉAL

Lir and Aébh welcomed a fine pair of twins, Aodh and Fionnuala. And Sídh Finnachadh was full of joy and laughter again. Bodhbh was very fond of his grandchildren, as were all who looked upon them. The Children of Lir were noted for their merriment and beauty.

ONN

a cup   for her milk

a blade   for her meat

a cow is more valuable with a calf inside her

There is a story that I heard in childhood, that I have thought of, time and time again, as the years stretched out, behind me and in front of me. It is the tale of Miach, who was the son of Dian Cecht, the healer, and by all accounts he was a better class of healer than his father and tried many new approaches beyond herbs. He had a special interest in people who had lost body parts and, in the course of his work, encountered a young man who had but one eye in his head. Miach offered to put the eye of a cat in his head for him, that he might see with two eyes instead of one. The young man agreed, and Miach took the eye from the cat in his lap and used it to build a new eye for the man.

Aébh, I remember, was always worried about the cat in the story, asking what became of it. I don't remember the answers that she got. To win the trust of a cat is no small thing. It was in his lap. Close to him, petted and at ease. Until he needed part of it for something. And then it wasn't safe there anymore. I assume it lost its trust in people, that it bore a scar. Innocent creatures may not know precisely why we hurt them, but there is an instinct there to shy away and not to trust as easily again. If it survived, which it may not have done. Not everyone survives the hurts they bear.

Cruelty aside, Miach's hands were sure and his skill unmatched, and when he was finished working, he left the man with two sighted eyes in his head. But one of them was never satisfied. It noticed something off about the world. It wasn't right. Something wasn't right.

The stolen eye flicked endlessly to the movement of the birds in the trees, the dart of field mice in the grass, and the man's heart would beat faster in his chest with the excitement of it. When he needed to focus, it could not be relied on not to drift away in sleep or peer about in search of a lick of milk. Milk isn't good for cats but they still love it.

He could never be his own self by himself after that, the man who had been half-blind. The third eyelid would move across the inside of his new eye like a slimy little tongue, reminding him that there was a part of him that wasn't his. He would always have a part of something primal flickering inside him, wanting things that weren't in his best interests, things that he was not supposed to want.

I could see how, over time, that sort of thing would drive a person mad. Would tempt you to do harm to yourself. If only to escape, just for a moment.

When you hurt another creature, we like to think there is always a price to pay. There often isn't, but there was for Miach. He died young, slain by his own father in a fit of jealousy over his skill with healing. I don't know what blood price Dian Cecht paid for his kin-slaying, but the act was not the end of their rivalry. From Miach's corpse sprang three hundred and sixty-five herbs, which his sister painstakingly organised according to their purpose. And it would have been a useful sort of death, only Dian Cecht tore them all apart and spread them out, and his daughter did not complete the task a second time. And still, thousands of years later, there are illnesses that have no known cure, and a person might wonder what could have been if Dian Cecht had just left well enough alone.

Not many people can do that, though.

I couldn't. Though my eyes were mine, there was a stirring in me like a cat, or an inhuman thing. The sense of not belonging. Wanting something different for myself. What other people had, and more besides. Enough to ease the stretch inside my heart. To make me feel like I was good enough. That I belonged, and I would not be lonely.

Aébh's absence was not easy for either of us. It changed things between myself and Ailbhe and she threw herself more and more into being a warrior, and I into my looking and my learning. The space that yawned between us allowed me to develop my skill with magic somewhat, and though my heart was sore for the loss of what we three had been to each other, it did provide no small satisfaction to find a power that was my own.

The next time that we saw Aébh was a year to the day after the wedding took place. She and Lir had come to Bodhbh's fort at Sídh Femuin to present their children to the king. They spent two days, and it was a joy to see those babies, with their tufty pale hair and wide eyes. We let them lie out naked on the grass and Aébh sat with us, while the men spoke indoors, and it was as though she had never left, how close we were.

My sister looked exhausted, though still so young and beautiful that you'd have to know her well to see as much. Her dark eyes were sunk in her bright face a very little. She said that she had not envisioned it being so hard. Her body ached. Her breasts were stuck with milk and they felt heavy, swollen, all the time, like two big boils to lance. Lir was kind, but she was tired, she was so very tired. We had very many questions for her, but she rested her head upon my lap and fell asleep. When she woke up, Ailbhe told her it would be easier soon, that the children would be weaned, and they would surely learn to sleep. Aébh nodded, but I had studied the shape of her, the slow tilt of her head. That smile that didn't meet those dark, deep eyes.

'I have many blessings,' my sister told us. And we nodded, looking at the babes' soft, fat legs.

I reached a finger out. Fionnuala grasped it.

'I too have many blessings,' Ailbhe said, rubbing a fresh scar, 'but that does not prevent the darker side of life. I wish it only made the good taste sweeter.'

I looked at them. The warrior and the mother, and I felt the love swell in my heart.

'She is a fine daughter, Aébh,' I told her. 'And he a fine son. Is Lir not pleased?'

'He is,' she said. 'I work hard to ensure it. This face I wear with you both, now, in private, is not a face I ever wear with him.'

'Similar to Bodhbh.' I thought of our foster-father, how much and how little he knew us, valued us.

'Yes,' Aébh said. 'He delights in me. In the shape of me. The sound of my sweet voice, my merry laugh. My grace. In the children I have given him, will give him. And that is more than many people have.'

And then we spoke of other things. Of grievances that people within those walls had with each other. Of broken promises. I laid out all the pieces of gossip I had heard, like treasures from a bag, one after another.

When the men were finished, we had dressed in fine clothes, decorated ourselves with golden things. I had braided Ailbhe's hair in the way she liked the best, back from her face and tight against the scalp. Aébh looked impeccable, but something in her face made me afraid. She wore a purple fringed cloak, fastened with a large silver brooch in the shape of a leaping salmon. *Quickening*, I thought, and thrust my hand out, wide against her belly. She flinched, but let me examine. She was holding Aodh against her hip, and he was making little sucking motions with his mouth, all want, all hunger.

They will take everything she has, I thought. *And ask for more.*

It was too soon to be with child again. We both knew that.

'I couldn't ...' she began, and then trailed off. I wonder how she would have finished that. At the time I thought I understood.

I moved my hands against her stomach, womb. I closed my eyes and focused on the babies. On what the shape of them, the size could tell me. I had been honing my gifts for noticing, no longer using only eyes and ears. I reached with my awareness, hoping to offer some comfort. I felt the loss of her so keenly then, and she still in front of me.

'Your hands are cold, Aífe' she said, and I could feel the question underneath it.

'Twins again,' I said, 'two hungry lives.'

And something broke in me. My hope. My heart.

'Oh, Aébh ... they'll be the death of you.'

Her voice was fierce. 'They can't be. And they won't be. I need to stay here. So I can protect them. Watch them grow.'

A catch then, and I met her dark swan's eyes. She knew. We knew.

'Lir.' She swallowed. 'He will want another. You or Ailbhe.'

Ailbhe's face looked the same way that I felt, but I had put my mask on, working, working. Seeking something useful I could do. A way to help. Aébh was speaking, but I could only hear the rhythm of her words like water rushing all around my brain, consuming me. I couldn't ask her to repeat herself. The men arrived, as Ailbhe whispered fiercely that she promised. I nodded in agreement.

Later on, when Lir and Aébh had left, departing for the white walls of Sídh Finnachadh with their twins, born and unborn, Ailbhe told me what our sister had asked of us. 'Whichever one he chooses, please protect them.'

And I filled a little water-vessel, placed one hand on the earth beneath us and another on the rough stone of the walls and closed my eyes until I felt the warm hum of the Earth. And I kept Aébh in my mind, and focused on my love for her, and my desire for her to be safe and well and with us. And, knowing the futility of it, I asked the Earth to help Aébh in whatever way it could. To keep my sister safe, or ease her on her journey between worlds.

The stone was cold, and I could feel her death beneath my hands. I thought of that girl-baby, grasping at my finger, tightly, fiercely. The boy's jaw working, hungry as the Dagda for his porridge. And something hopeless swelled inside my heart.

SCÉAL

Aébh bore Lir another set of twins, two sons this time, Fiachra and Conn, but unfortunately she died bringing them into the world. Lir was alone again, and the children needed a mother. And so Bodhbh invited him to choose another wife from his two remaining daughters. Lir chose the second, Aífe. And for a time, the two of them were happy.

BEITH

in the stomach, hope and fear

are sisters

A person can do many things at once. Aébh was dead, but the world was still there, around me, and I had to stay in it and do the bidding of our foster-father, who wanted one of us to take her place. I washed my body till it gleamed with health, arranged my hair into nine loose tresses down my back. Ailbhe wove her hair into two locks of red-gold, and each tress a weaving of four twists with a globe at the end. We took our time with it. We made an effort. To please Bodhbh and to spare each other.

The news had reached us as the leaves began to fall. The dark came early. Aébh had passed from the realm of men into the Otherworld. She would live a life there, on the delightful plain, and when her time was finished, she would return to us in another form. No-one ever leaves the world, not fully. They just leave you. We were left behind.

And so were they. Those children. Aodh, Fionnuala and the two new babies. As healthy as my sister had been once, before she married Lir. Twins again, but this time perfect doubles of each other. The same small bodies and the same small faces. I had not much experience of twins, but for their brother and sister. But these babies were very different things. Two boys.

Their emotions, expressions mirrored the one to the other, and noises passed between them as though they were in dialogue. It was a curious, unsettling thing to see. I told myself it was my grief back then. That they were innocents. No reason to be scared.

But there was plenty reason to be scared. Just not of them. Lir's face was drawn, but his eyes were hungry when he came to present my foster-father with his grandsons. I could see his eyes taking everything in. Paying particular attention to Ailbhe and myself, as he spoke to the king about how badly every child needed a woman's hand to guide them through the world. I could see so clearly what he meant. He had been inconvenienced by her death. And it incensed me. I pictured a cloud of blood above his head, pulsing and enlarging until it consumed the throne, the roof, the walls.

I thought of the Dagda again, him and his porridge, maw open, shoving it into him with force, so hungry that when he reached the bottom of the cauldron, he kept going. Eating metal, gravel, eating earth. Filling himself tight as a water-skin and wanting more and taking more again.

I was a girl who spent an inordinate amount of time longing for all that I could not have, and I became a woman who wanted things. Who always wanted things. And maybe that was why this man disgusted me. The greed of him mirrored the greed of me. My biggest flaw, as I perceived it then. The stones are silent now, in this big world, and I have learned more about myself.

SAILLE

creation is no small feat, listen I am

a person

or the memory of one

I know this

I am telling you a story

The world is an old tongue softly whispered, but the sound of it is getting hoarser. I can feel my own thoughts getting away from me, not as they did before, when I was younger, in a tumult, but atrophying, fading into static, stony nothing. I am becoming glimpses of myself.

I have thought, before, of putting who I am, who I have been and am, into something like words. Keening on the air will only get you so far in this world. There are too many voices to pierce through.

Please protect them.

Both of us grieving, both of us wanting to do what we could. To do our best to help our sister's children, to protect the other one from a loveless marriage to a hungry man. I felt it should be me. I was quiet, but had a kind of power. A sense of people. I could ferret certain secrets out. And there were ways, small ways back then, to make the world bend to my will. Nothing like what druids could accomplish with their rituals. But something I had gleaned myself, from who I was, as well as from the watching and the learning. I think that sort of magic, the more instinctive sort, comes easier to women than to men. The land itself is feminine, you see. The water and the earth. And once you learn the way to ask, it listens. And then it's just a case of improving your vocabulary. I was proud. I still am proud of what I learned in spite of them, just not of what it led to.

One of the great stories people tell, the one about the bulls, was told by a ghost. Called back from the dead to share the poetry of what he'd lived. I am not a ghost. I am something else. I do not think there is another thing of what I am, and if there is I have never met one or heard of one. I had water in me from the cradle, but there was fire there as well. And perhaps that led to my downfall, but perhaps it's why I still have keen eyes in my head, a memory for detail. When I encounter humans, which sometimes happens now, but very rarely, I like to think that I can read them still. Who we are and all the things we want, they do not change that much. The shape of them, the picture in our heads, might warp and shift, but the longing is the same.

The longing in me then was very big. I didn't see it, really. But Lir did. He learned to use it well. Fair play to him. When he took me to Sídh Finnachadh, his home, with its curved white walls and roof thatched with bird feathers, I marvelled. I had known that it was famed for its beauty, but often that has little to do with the actual beauty of a thing, more to do with someone's reputation. I smiled at Lir, as we approached the hill. It was steep, but manageable. The horses were straining, and I suggested that we get out, looking at the beaded sweat, coiled muscle. Lir shook his head. 'Let them work,' he told me. 'Everything here has to earn its keep.'

I forced a smile upon my face and tossed my hair. And I remembered that.

As he intended.

We coupled that night and it felt strange to know another person's body in that manner. My sister's husband too. I pressed my face against the wolf-pelt and wondered what Aébh would think. We hadn't spoken of that side of things. She had belonged to Lir, pressed into his hand like a brooch. Lir kissed my face. He called me precious, lovely. He held me in his arms. And I can see the things I should have seen. I was sharp. I knew how people were. What he was. But I had never been held like that before. And I wanted to be precious, to be lovely. Not just the second sister in the line.

That little hand reached out and stroked Lir's chest. And he was not so old. We live long lives, our people. He carried his years well. His hair was white, but his skin was smooth, his eyes sea-green, sea-grey. They shifted and they changed with every mood. I noticed that. I noticed everything about my Lir, but now it became more delight than inventory. I was interested in him, in who he was. And I craved the same from him.

He asked me questions and I told him answers, more information than I needed to, just to keep him looking on me, talking. It wasn't the physical side of things, though that was part of it. Skin to skin is powerful. They place babes on their mothers when they're born. To know they're not alone in this strange place. Some enchantments work best in your skin as well, with nothing separating you from the elements. I suppose

I'm always naked now, in a sense. But it's different. When you aren't human, nudity is no cause for concern.

Lir sent Bodhbh many magnificent gifts in gratitude for my hand. He had done the same for Aébh, but smaller. I watched treasure boxes, baskets and one hundred and fifty gleaming swords leave Sídh Finnachadh, and he told me, 'You're worth all that and more.'

I tossed my hair and told him that I knew. He laughed at that. I liked surprising Lir. I had begun to think of him before I thought of myself. I had begun to enjoy being paid for. Instead of scaring me, it made me feel safe.

How little I knew then.

But were I back within the white walls of Sídh Finnachadh, to live my life again, I do not know how I could change my fate and come out well. My foster-father's finest musician, Fer Tuinne, could play well enough to enchant a hall. Well enough, it was said, that he could soothe a warrior in battle-fury or a woman in the throes of giving birth to peaceful sleep. Make them forget the anger, or the pain. And for a time, my new home was like that. But music fades, and there are things you can't escape entirely.

The children themselves were kept from me, I realised, for the first while to give Lir a chance to spend time with me. To make me his. He kissed them at night before they went to sleep, and in the morning to greet them. He held them often. And as the days I spent in my new home stretched into weeks, I too began to do so. They resembled Aébh so closely, particularly the youngest ones.

The children, Fionnuala, Aodh, Conn and Fiachra, who would become known as the Children of Lir, were, I shall remind you, not his only children. He had gotten sons on his first wife, and he would get more on the women after me for all his grief. All in all, Lir had more than a hundred and fifty children in his time. He acknowledged them all, delighted in his potency and how it made him seem to other men. Were he alive now, and perhaps somewhere he is, in another body and another life, he would have other ways to demonstrate how much more he was than other people. A soul like his would never be satisfied with what he had. Never completely. If I had been born in a different body, perhaps I would not have been unlike him. I collected thoughts like those, in the early stages of our marriage. I longed for love, and I would turn whatever small kind thing he felt for me into it, if I had to work my fingers to the bone. I listened to his plans for the children we would have. Our fine strong sons. His women, he told me, generally produced boy-children and, perhaps because of the rarity of her, he adored Fionnuala.

Fionnuala, when I arrived, was very young, a chubby, boisterous thing with down-soft hair and big dark eyes. She noticed everything and had a mania for eating berries. If you found yourself popping one into your mouth, she would appear, demanding her small portion. She was a queen already, I always said to Lir. She watched people like I did, but unlike me, she told everyone exactly what she'd heard and instantly demanded explanations. She was the most charming child I think I've ever encountered, but she could vex me like nobody else. So many questions. And the strength of her love for her brother, Aodh, and the other two as well was something powerful. Even as a child, with all a child's small cruelties, I never saw her raise her hand to them, except in play. Perhaps she felt the absence of a mother. I wish that I could have been more like Aébh. Or that my sister lived to raise her children proudly and with love. When I looked at them, it was with fondness, but the deep well that mothers are supposed to feel was never really there. I would not have jumped in front of a sword for them. I would not have gone without sufficient food so they could eat. The things I would have done for Aébh, for Ailbhe, without a moment's thought did not extend to these peculiar children. I was their father's wife, their mother's sister. I softened, but not by much. They were my job, not my vocation. It was a strange position to be in, and though I was colder than I would wish myself to be, I did appreciate their individual qualities. Lir really did make beautiful children. If we had had a child, with both our wants all mingled up together, his warrior's blood and my skill with magic, it could have been a world-changing creature. For good or ill. But I have wandered off again, I see. I will tell you now about my soft sweet boy. My little Aodh, who was quieter than his sister, but no less special. There was a vulnerability to him that made me want to shield him from the world. Fionnuala's shadow, he always held a small piece of purple cloth in his hand. When he felt that it would go unnoticed he would raise the cloth to his face and suck his thumb and smell it. It was grey and pocked with various stains. I tried several times to steal it from him as he slept, for the purposes of washing, but the ever-vigilant Fionnuala stopped me.

'Don't take our mother's cloak,' she said. And I looked at the fraying mess inside his hand, ratted with rubs, and remembered the bright cloaks they had worn the day my sister left us for Sídh Finnachadh. Swallowing, I apologised to her and fled the room before she saw my tears.

I wanted to protect them for my sister, but who they were also deserved protection. I started sharing little bits of Aébh with them, so they could know what sort of person she had been when she was small like them. The games she liked to play. The boldnesses she'd done when we were little. Her favourite songs, the way she liked to dance. I asked Lir where the cloak had gone, and replaced Aodh's fabric with another. I used what magic skills I had to clean the original, without removing Aébh's scent. I concealed this from Lir. I don't know why, exactly. Perhaps something to do with his dislike for Aodh's self-soothing habit. Perhaps because, in spite of everything, I needed something wholly of my own. It matters little why, in any case. Except that if he'd known, things might have gone a little differently. Worse for me, but better for the children. Perhaps. Perhaps.

There are so many threads to worry at.

SCÉAL

Soon, Aífe began to feel very jealous of the attention Lir lavished upon his children. She wanted all of his love for herself. Resentment and darkness grew in her heart. She pretended to have an illness and took herself to bed for a year.

AILM

I was beautiful   I was no longer beautiful   I was difficult

Many goddesses have more than one face. The Morrigan, the queen of phantoms, can be a crow, a panic or a red-haired woman. Before a battle, she may send her allies handfuls of blood to let them know her hunger is on their side. And she can be an eel, a wolf, a red cow without horns.

People can be like that too.

I was.

The face I wore with Lir was more and more like what I thought he wanted and less like me. I was the gold in the brooch and he was the jewel. I was the scabbard and he was the sword. I was the crown and he was the head that wore it. My function was to make him seem more. More powerful, more imposing, more envied. My beauty was not that great. It never was. However, I was young, my skin was smooth. My flesh was soft. I did the best I could.

I sat beside him in the central room of the fortress, as we ate in the evenings. I followed him, draped myself softly on his arm and gazed at him adoringly. He did not always slow his step to meet with mine, but I told myself that was to be expected. He was a chieftain, and my job was to please him. I have had time, whole swathes of lonely, uninterrupted time, to contemplate the things I knew of him. When I lived those days, I did not have the luxury of hindsight, or of foresight.

When I corrected him, gently, and he said in the earshot of his people, 'What a keen mind my wife has, never was any woman more pleasing,' I thought it meant he valued me, but he only valued the appearance of valuing me. Which was too much distance for me to walk from the love I felt for him, the shine I felt when I could see his face.

Lir was a wonderful man. Kind to dogs and servants, fierce in battle. A loving father and a devoted husband. He did not deserve what came to pass. That is one story.

I craved his attention, and Lir craved power and became angry when he did not get the things he wanted. This anger he took out in the ways he could afford to do. He did not like to hear the word no. And for all that he pretended to admire my intelligence, he resented it.

I learned how to please him.

Silence was one of the ways.

Lir liked his women to listen to him.

And listen well.

Fortunately, I had no small skill with this. I took to the task of retaining his love for me as though I were preparing to be initiated into a band of warriors. I worked on my body and my brain. I learned the correct things to do, and did them often, until it became second nature, and who I had been before was as a shadow to who I had to be to make him want me. If it had worked, I might be a shadow still, wisping my way behind him in the Otherworld. I thought that that was what I wanted too, you see. The alternative was never knowing love. And I had had a taste of being precious. And, though I was more stone than jewel, I could smooth my edges, chip away.

I started bathing with special herbs and schooled myself on ways I could contrive to make my better features more pronounced. To have other people admire my beauty. Other people's eyes were important to Lir. Sídh Finnachadh was known as the most beautiful and finest *sídh*. And it was a splendid place. Lir never refused any guest with a mouth for eating, knowing well that same mouth would later be used to sing the praises of Sídh Finnachadh. Thatched with bird feathers, for crying out loud. Smooth white marble, shining, flashing walls. Golden windows. Lir would have done very well in this world now, I think. He had a gift for shaping the way people thought of him.

And over time, and probably too much of it, I began to wonder if the great woe Lir had felt with the death of his first wife, Emer, and the great woe he had felt in the wake of Aébh's passing was, in some way, a performance. A story he was telling of himself. Your heart only breaks that badly if you are the pinnacle of husbands, married to the best of wives.

I, ever an unlikely candidate for the 'best of wives', began to use that brain he liked telling other people he was proud of to take stock of this husband that I had. And once I had taken that step away, and looked at him and thought about him critically, I found I wanted him no less, I loved him no less, but I feared for myself and my future more. Survival seemed, one way or another, most unlikely. I could not compete with ghosts, gilded to perfection by their deaths.

I became, or remembered that I had always been, a bit suspicious. It built up slowly, stone by little stone.

If you loved someone that deeply, and wisdom and kindness told you to leave her bed alone until she'd healed, would you then resolve yourself to get more children on her?

I wondered sometimes what had killed his first wife. It had seemed very convenient at the time, in the way that convenient things seemed to happen around my foster-father. Lir was denied the kingship, he was angry, left the place and went home to Sídh Finnachadh. Bodhbh was advised that Lir could be a threat. Bodhbh had the kingship and three young fosterlings. Emer, Lir's wife of many years, the mother of his grown-up children, took ill that very night and died three days later. Was it one man's wisdom or another's anger that took her?

Of course, convenient things happen all the time.

And if you tell a story often enough, it becomes the thing that's written down.

Take the story of Oisín and Niamh, for example. He abducted her, and her father the king of Munster came with hundreds of warriors to bring her home. She stood upon a hill away from them, and as she saw them and their approach towards her, her heart burst out of her chest, they say, with shame, and all her serving women followed suit. Shame doesn't do that to a heart, but a spear will do a fine job of it, if you've one handy. The story was that they fell in love and eloped. That her father, incensed at her disobedience, followed after them, and her fatal shame came as his warriors assembled on the hill behind them ready for the conflict. Nobody bothered reading in between the lines too much. She was just a silly girl who couldn't keep her legs closed or her heart inside her ribcage. And, to keep people from reading in between the lines, they mixed her up with another story and another. They put her on a magic horse and brought her back from the dead to carry Oisín west with her.

The Fianna gave her father the weight in silver and gold of every woman dead upon that hill. You don't pay a blood price unless you're guilty. And Finn, tight as a tick, never paid anything he didn't have to.

You cannot trust a story.

Even mine.

Remember that.

Be careful.

I am seeking something like the truth. A truth, at least *my* truth. And I don't want to daub Lir's name with mud to show you how I shine. I am not a shining creature. I am an ugly thing and part of me has always been an ugly thing. A sneak. A child who liked attention, power. A woman who looked jealously at love that wasn't for her and resented it.

I thought, or hoped, that joy was possible for me, for us.

That I could make him mine.

That time and want and love would be enough.

And, like poor Niamh, my heart swelled in my chest. But it stayed there, fat with stupid hope, and kept on beating.

It didn't happen quickly, the shift from wife to burden. I did my best to cling on for dear life to what I had. I became a shadow, to listen to him. I did not care for killing things, though from the way I am remembered you'd swear I was the cruellest of my cruel race. And I *was* cruel. It is no small thing, to hurt a child. I gave to them, as well. Before I hurt them. My time and my energy, if not the full of my heart. I fed them, watered them, played with them, sang to them, listened to their sorrows and their joys, cleaned up their waste and vomit, healed their sickness. And still they loved their father more than me.

Sure, I could hardly blame them.

So did I.

As I began to see him for himself, my love for him did not decrease at all. I knew, deeply and fiercely, what it was to crave attention. I wanted to give him everything. I wanted to play *ficheall* with him. To walk together across his lands. To ride out with the hunt. I wanted him to sleep beside me when he didn't have to. Most of all, I wanted him to love me again, the way I thought he had. I wanted happiness that lasted.

It was almost a relief when he was off hunting or making war. He was not in front of me to amplify my failures. All the ways I was not good enough. The Invaders were holding their own, and more besides, against our forces. And the fear of what life would be like, if we were ousted from this land that was our own, added to the fierceness with which I clutched at Lir and at the life we shared. I wanted to be happy while I could be.

We visited Bodhbh the Red's house often, and he spent time with the children, as did Ailbhe. They took pleasure in watching them grow, and the children took pleasure in the attention and care of their aunt and grandfather. I could have taken pleasure in the respite, I think, but I did not. I was still on show. I needed to perform smiles and caring, even when I longed to sleep, to scream. I would sit sometimes in silence as they played in the central chamber, before Bodhbh's throne, the way I had when I was a little girl, and I would wonder if any of them would notice if I disappeared. If something happened to me, and I was no longer there.

Would Lir swallow up Ailbhe? He might have met his match, I thought. Ailbhe was magnificent. She had grown into an exceptional warrior, and her skill with sword and spear were well known. She had become one of the Nine who stayed by our foster-father's side now to protect him. It was the first time a woman had been given this honour. Bodhbh looked the same as he had when we were children, and I wondered how long he had looked that age, that way. How old he even was. As old as the world itself, or just a little younger, it sometimes seemed. Our foster-mother, Ban, would sit with him, and she would ask me polite questions out of interest. What food the children liked, details about Sídh Finnachadh. How Lir had managed to acquire all those feathers for the thatch. It had to be magic, did it not? I nodded. He got warriors out hunting and they tore the wings from birds and brought them home, armful by armful, but the hundreds of wings that they brought back would not, by themselves, be enough. And the colours in the thatch were Otherwordly. There was more to Lir than met the eye.

Magic was a talent that my people had, back when our connection to the land was a living, breathing thing. Lir had an affinity for water, and he would often go for a swim when he needed to think. He would emerge the better for it. It was one of the things I hoped we had in common. I would sometimes go out to the lake as well, and lie on my back, staring up at the sky above me and wondering what lay beyond the clouds, how vast it was, how lonely. Where the stars would hide till night time came. And I would feel cupped by the water around the edges of my body and grounded by the knowledge of the earth that was my home underneath the surface, cupping everything, like a kind hand.

I also liked to walk in the wilderness, and barefoot. That is how I came into the power. By listening to the land until it spoke to me, and told me things. And when I used what it had given me so ill, that was a betrayal on my part.

It was unusual for a noblewoman to walk alone, but I needed time away from other people, in the air. And if there were ever anything, man or beast, who tried to hurt me, I would hurt them back with every bit of skill that Dechtaire and Smól had taught me, and with every bit of fire that was my own. I did not seek conflict out, but I would not back down from things that needed doing. Lir didn't like it, and he made that clear. And I, who would have fought a wolf bare-handed to protect myself, stayed inside and gave away another piece of who I was.

There is an old story people tell about a seven-year-old child who took up arms and killed a guard dog. That boy grew up to kill a lot of men, and we still sing his praises as a hero. When the frenzy of battle came upon this warrior, his face changed. His eyes bulged and the cables in his neck became pronounced. It is a sort of element in itself, the bloodlust. Sometimes he was thrown in vats of cold water, time and time again, until the desire to murder abated.

This is fine.

This is a noble thing.

And what I did is not.

There are accepted ways to hurt a person.

And I will readily admit that I transgressed, but I wonder at the transgressions of others, which seem to meet with far less severe punishment. I am what I am. And I did what I did. No good will come of raging at what is.

This child in the story, Setanta, when he took his hurl and followed his uncle to a stranger's house, he thought it would be safe. They had forgotten him. The dog approached, knowing what its job was, and, unable to distinguish between a stranger and an unexpected guest, it went to savage him and it was slaughtered. Its master mourned for it, and the child's name changed. He was for ever linked to what he'd done. The Hound of Culainn. His atonement, as a replacement guard dog, until another could be found and trained.

We all have different stories, and brutality is easier to take from those who matter.

People know what bloodied hands look like.

The price there is to pay.

If I had been a favoured daughter, perhaps my fate would have been different.

If Lir had loved me back, or been respectful of the love I gave him.

The children did no wrong.

They did no wrong.

They grew, they sang, they thrived. But, over time, I felt myself waning and becoming more unsure of the edges of my body, of the places that I bled into the world. I was like a badly woven shawl. I wasn't as good as other people, somehow. And all it would take was one tug on the right small twist of cloth.

I'd come apart.

That small hand that I had felt before, reaching out, was far away from me, grasping at something I could never have and I felt almost like it touched that thing and, in doing so, was ripped out at the root. There was a hole inside me, a chasm. And when I looked at myself, I hated what I saw. It was around this time that Lir sensed my separation from him, my lack of effort more, and it grated upon him. My hair unbrushed and my face unwashed. Crusts of sleep in my eyes and black dirt on my feet. Blood and scars dotting my arms and face.

I looked more crone than noblewoman.

Which was meet.

Lir decided that the kindest course of action was to give me what I needed. What every woman needed. What Lir liked the best about his wives. A baby of my own.

I could barely take care of myself.

And there he was on top of me. Too heavy and too much. What I deserved. I stared at the fine thatch of bird feathers. But I was more than this. I couldn't function. He kept his eyes closed. He did not call me precious.

I was not precious and his face was grim.

I could not see a way to shield myself.

While all of this was going on with me, the children were left to Lir and the castle. They began to shun me. And I could see why. I reeked. I shrank. When people spoke to me, I replied haltingly as though I was an animal who had been granted the power of speech but was unsure of the structure or meaning of words. I only registered half what they said. I had been sharp, and now I was made stupid by a grief I could neither fathom nor explain. I stopped enjoying food, and mead, and stories. I stopped listening for things. When I went into the wilderness to speak to the land, I would place my hands flat on the ground in the centre of a circle of stones. I would wait to hear the flow of water beneath earth. For the mother's voice to speak to me.

And she would not.

Or I could not, broken as I was, begin to hear her.

And that feeling, that I couldn't even pray.

That nobody would listen, or care.

It widened the grief within me, and soon I was swallowed whole.

I remember little after that.

They found me in the forest, and my hair was wild and I was sobbing.

They put me in a room all by myself, and there I stayed.

There, for a year, I stayed.

SCÉAL

When Aífe emerged, she was much changed. And she called her four step-children to her, and demanded that the chariot be yoked. She would take them to the Sídh of Femuin, to visit their grandfather. The children, fearful of this sudden change in her, were reluctant to go, particularly Fionnuala, who had foreseen that nothing good would come of it.

QUERT

when you

go   all

alone   into

the

wilderness

you bring it back with you when you return

I don't know exactly when I ceased to be myself and became something else: a disappointment, a creature who would not give Lir a baby, who could not give Lir a baby. Not in the state that I was in. I know that he wanted the perfect life. All the symbols of the greatest chieftain. Endless infants streaming out of me like sheep that people count to sleep. When I loved him, even when I loved him, I found myself seeking the proper herbs, preparing them and taking them. There were so many pieces of myself I gave up readily, but I managed that much. I wanted time. I wanted to be sure I would be good at it. And I could see that I was not, that I had a short temper and a love of time spent by myself that would not serve an infant particularly well. I saw how I was with the children and did not want any child of mine to be treated that way. It wasn't that I became angry and jealous because I failed to give Lir a child, it was that I was too aware of my own anger and jealousy to want to. I was a woman grown, and married, but I still felt like the small girl I had been who missed the parents she could scarce remember. Who longed for home, or something like a home. How could I give what I had never known?

I thought, at first, that time would change my mind. That as the years passed, I would wake up ready, able, right. As fertile as Brigid, as strong as Macha. I was young, closer to the age of the children of Lir than to Lir himself. I was hungry for love and for adventure. I liked the newness of our lives. I liked feeling like I mattered, ordering the servants about, dropping things so they would pick them up. Sometimes I would strike one of them. Just to see the mark it made on their skin. The swallowed anger.

The impact I could have.

I did not tell you all of this before.

I am not a good person.

None of my good fortune brought me pleasure. Or not enough to stop me doing wrong. I think if I had been the high king himself, I would still have been unhappy.

And not as good at hiding it as Bodhbh.

As it became clear to me that Lir did not return my favour any more, that we were man and wife, but that he would divorce me, send me back, if at all he could, if it were not a failing, I lashed out more. I tore up things that I didn't need to tear. I spat inside his shoes so he would put his feet in them and hate me. And he just brushed it all aside, as though I were a minor inconvenience. A silly girl who couldn't do her job. I wanted him to warm me, to help me through this life we were building together, and it would not have taken very much. Apparently I wasn't worth the pains.

And I felt useless

But I was worse than useless.

I was malicious.

What good can you say of a woman who has hurt a child?

I am unnatural.

My rage felt like a balm in comparison to the numbness that followed it. All the petty things that I had done before were sucked away. I lost myself. My chamber was where I lived. I didn't care to leave it, and when I considered that perhaps I should, it was frightening. The thought of being in the world was too much to bear. And sometimes Lir would come, or the children, and they would say things to me, and I would look at them as though I didn't know them. I did know them, I did. But in an abstract way. This was Lir, I thought. Lir was my husband. What was Lir saying to me? This was Fionnuala. She was a clever, brave girl. My sister's daughter. This was Aodh, who was her twin. He was sweet and beautiful. This was Conn. Conn shuffled before he crawled, and loved to bathe with Lir. This was Fiachra. Fiachra was very interested in cattle. I remembered the details. I did. But from a distance. It was as though I was standing with my two feet on a hill, watching people that I'd only heard of approaching me. As though they were figures in a story.

Which, I suppose, is just what they became.

And I did that.

If the children had taken me by the hand and led me from where I was to somewhere kinder, perhaps things would have gone differently. That would have been a pleasant story. Maybe not as memorable, but I would have come out of it better. They didn't, though. Why would they have? I was just pieces of a person strung together. And they had learned from their father how little I mattered. Why would they have reached out for a hand that found it easier to hurt than help? But no-one tried to help me. Though, perhaps, I would not have allowed it if they had.

I didn't trust other people.

I was right not to trust them.

I curled in the corner, sometimes banging my head against the wall to feel the impact of it. And perhaps things would have continued in that vein, until I worked up the courage to successfully destroy myself, but I had a dream one night, or it could have been the daytime, there was no light inside the room, so time was hard to gauge, and it meant little. It wasn't where you would expect a noblewoman to be. But I had not been acting like a noblewoman. I had been acting like an animal. And so I got my pen. I gasped awake and the images reeled in my head.

An apple tree.

A sword.

A hand.

An apple cut in two.

My eye inside.

Gazing out in horror.

The apple closed and given to Lir.

Lir biting it, and blood staining the corners of his mouth.

I had the sense that these were not the apples in the east of the world that would heal any sadness on you and cure vexation. These apples were not for healing. They were for something else. My eye inside. I placed my two hands on the rough stone of the wall and breathed in the smell of my own filth and tried to push past sensation to a deeper sense.

She had left me over a year ago, the Earth.

I had called and called to her again.

Had given blood and tears.

She wouldn't hear me.

But now, at last, I felt a sense of something pushing back.

And an unpleasant clarity with it. Lir could not or would not divorce me, or let me divorce him, because of the alliance with Bodhbh. It would be a clear public rejection of the high king, at such a delicate and brutal time for our people. That would not sit well with the enemies of Lir, who still thought that he could be a threat to Bodhbh. Who had, after the kingship was decided, encouraged my foster-father to kill him.

Instead he had decided to kill me.

But it was not exactly that. The eye. There was something that they were going to do, and it would hurt me. Change me back into the thing they wanted me to be. And it would hurt. I would still be inside there, hurting, hurting. Being eaten, piece by little piece.

She gave me that knowledge, the Earth. And I was grateful.

Because it gave me back my fire. My rage.

My ingenuity, if not my reason.

I was incandescent. And what I wanted was to humiliate these men. To hurt these men. To take from them something publicly. And in a way they would not be able to ignore or fix. And I wanted them to look me in the eye, and know that I had done it. That I had a power that was not tied to my father, or my husband, but was my own entirely. Something they could not take from me.

My eyes then settled upon the Children of Lir.

Who had done me no harm, and came from the body of the sister I had loved and who had loved me. That mattered not. They had looked on me with disgust. Their presence had been used to shame me for my childlessness. Their birth had killed the sister that I loved. But most of all, they were a thing he prized. And they would pay.

UILLEANN

in my

graceful

pain

was nothing

my wounds were not white and there

Plans don't just form. They're made. I didn't simply stalk outside one day and decide to do what I did. It wasn't easy to leave that room, to go outside into the world again. There was so much of it, and people would see me and know where I had been and hate me for it. I began, at first, to leave the *sidh* at night, to visit the wilderness. The trees, the lake. I would load myself with stones and wade into the water until it reached my neck. I would stand there, sensing the pulse and rush of life around me, of the leaping little fish and the weed like mermaids' hair, winding and floating. And I would hear the hum of insect wings, the little splash of something diving in, perhaps a frog. The wind filtering through the trees themselves, older and wiser far than I felt I would ever be. I would sometimes take one more step, and another, until the water of the lake was right beneath my nostrils, ready, there, to send me on my way.

I would stay inside the water, trying to remember how to stay in the world. I would think of all that had been taken from me, and all that had been given to me. I would count my good fortune with my bad. I would reach out towards the island that we came from, to my father's fort. To Oillill and Éabha, and I would picture their faces. Always, it seemed they were just the faces of Dechtaire and Smól, our hired mothers. I would think of Bodhbh, his wife and his children, all his children, twenty-seven sons and as many daughters dotted across Ireland like messenger birds, and I would think of how easy it had been for him to give Aébh to Lir, and how easy in the wake of her death to replace her with myself, who could never replace her. I would think of Lir's hands winding through the thick fur of his hounds, which were as silver-grey and rough as the hairs upon his head and beard. I would think of his face smiling at his children's sleeping forms, their breath collecting in the air like druidic mist. I would think of all the mysteries I could have uncovered if I had been allowed to be a druid, instead of being traded like a beast. I would think of Lir's face above me in the night, his eyes closed tightly now, thinking, no doubt, of the sons that I would give him were I not such a disappointment. And I would feel the water of the lake warming up with the fierce anger inside me then. That I would be naught but a hole to fill, a door to close.

I would think of the children's faces too, confused and mocking. Fionnuala shying away from me on the rare occasions I left the room, for fear she'd have to speak to me, to smell me. They were ashamed. I would not be ashamed. I could not be, not with such a bright anger coursing through my veins like a hound maddened and exhilarated by the smell of quarry. I was tired of counting all my faults, of being silent and dismissed. I drank the mead of fury with a thirst on me as though it were the only worldly thing that could make me strong enough to tolerate what life is without screaming. And after a time, my anger taught me things. Where to find the grave of Lir's old druid, Diangalach, so I might desecrate it, disinter his corpse and steal the bones of his left hip, that I might whittle and shape them into a wand of power. My anger did that for me in the night.

The days were different too. I could still feel the void in me, but it no longer hurt. Now it was just a part of who I was, a constant reminder to myself that I was different from other people.

That, in spite of my good fortune, I was not grateful.

That, in spite of my capacity for love, nobody loved me.

Why would they have? I could not do the basic things that people are supposed to do. I couldn't make my husband love me back. I couldn't bring myself to bear his children. I couldn't do the work of raising Fionnuala, Aodh, Fiachra and Conn without growing tired of their voices, their demands. Without resenting that every night my husband chose to share his children's bed until they fell asleep, and that every morning, he would leave me cold to warm them as they woke. Which, perhaps, was why I used the night to my own ends, abandoning his *sídh*, like he had abandoned my company. Listening to myself, my own raw rage, louder even than my sorrow had been. No-one asked me how I was, no-one cared. There were no other voices to drown out. It was only me, by myself alone. That was all I had.

I suppose that Lir's well-acknowledged love for his children was a sort of assertion of his power too. Reminding them that they belonged to him. I am remembered as Lir's other wife. Their story, when it is told, is called the Fate of the Children of

Lir, or the Sorrow of the Children of Lir, or just the Children of Lir. We are all defined, even more than a thousand years later, by what we were to him or did to him. But I think what defines me most is that split from my parents and my home when we were babies. The hunger and the anger started then. Before I had a word to put on it, a way to explain it to myself. Before I knew what it could do, not just to me, but to others. To innocents.

Aengus Óg, Bodhbh's brother, was, they later said, a god of love. Gods were people then, and people are many things at once – kind and cruel all jumbled up together. At the time, when everyone had their little bits of magic, the world was different. Quieter, in a way, but more things spoke. And we were trained to listen. It was a bit like having an ear for music. Some people when they hear a strain on the air can go back home and pick it out on dulcimer, piano or any other thing they like to play. The flute. The harp. It seems that I have drifted.

I am sorry.

This is hard to look at directly, even now.

I am going to tell you another story so I don't have to tell you mine.

And maybe, when it is finished, I will be closer to the strength I need. The things I did. But I will say this. I had, even without training, a wonderful ear for magic power. And I had a greed for information too. I had been watching what worked and didn't work for years. Listening intently to the druids, even when they didn't know I was there. That doesn't always work out well for people.

The River Shannon was a curious girl, Sionann, who tried to eat some hazelnuts and gain wisdom, and the waters rose up to swallow her whole. They had placed a curse on that place to hoard their sacred knowledge for themselves. I would have done the same and suffered the same fate.

Knowledge is tempting.

But it can be a weapon in your hand.

If you apply it without compassion.

Let me return to the story of Aengus Óg and not be tying myself in knots to prevent the side of me I hate the most (of all my hateful sides) getting held up to the light, examined. I have been silent for so long, and it is not small to open my mouth and begin to speak again. It reminds me that there was a time when I belonged here, before the civilisation I was part of fell to dust, like the bones of old, old children.

Aébh, as I have said to you before, reminded me of a swan, with her large body and her slender neck. And Aengus Óg fell in love with a similarly graceful woman, Caer, who appeared in his dreams. She reached for him and he could not forget her. When I picture Caer, I picture Aébh, and it is hard to look at her directly.

Aengus needed help, and so he went to Bodhbh. My foster-father, always keen for someone to owe him a favour, managed to find her. She was chained up with a hundred and fifty other girls, linked in pairs, beside a lake somewhere in Tipperary.

Aengus followed Caer back to her home, and her father told him that, in spite of the chains, she was very powerful and he had no control over her. She chose to spend one year as a woman and one year as a swan. And Aengus won her love by recognising her in her swan form. And he turned into one as well, so it could be the two of them together. And his kisses were little songbirds in the air.

It isn't bad, sometimes, to change your shape.

Like all the big ones, birth and death and love.

They don't flatten everyone.

When I was sick, Fiachra and Conn made fun of me. Fionnuala laughed with them, as did Lir, and Aodh told them to stop it. That I couldn't help the way I was. And I held that grievance in me. And every cry they'd cried. Every pull of hair. Every little moment when they had turned from me, and every moment when they had chosen Lir. Lir who couldn't love me, but loved them. Lir whose eyes rested on Fionnuala as if she were the most beautiful, most graceful, brilliant thing. Which she was. There was a strength and power in that girl. They say sometimes that young thorns are the sharpest. Kindness is a reach for any child. It takes time, I think, to realise that the people who reared you are people and not a class of servant or boss. And I don't blame them for hating me. I was loathsome. I even loathed myself.

I am racking my brain trying to think of other paths to take. Of worse people than me. And there were plenty of them. It was a warlike, vengeful time. People killed each other, cursed each other, let old friends die from spite. Schemed and stole and slaughtered. The wilderness was in the country then, in the land and in the people too. Tree by tree it has been leached from us.

The world is brutal in a different way now. A way I do not even understand. There are so many changes, quick as the wings on a hummingbird.

And I am still here, buried in the past.

I can't forget.

I do hate it, this looking at the things that I have done. Seeing what other people see, have seen. And I can tell you where I came from, where I went, what hurt inside my heart that day, but I can't tell you the lies that I would love to be the truth.

I cannot tell you that I left the room that day and braided my hair and washed my face and went to the Children of Lir with a bright smile and a warm heart and said to them, 'I'm sorry. Let us go to visit my foster-father. I will show you things your mother liked. She was my sister, as you know. I want you to know that I carry love for her inside my heart and with it love for you. And nothing that you could ever do would make me stop loving you. Even if we fight, even if I break, even if nine hundred years or more pass, that love, her love and mine all mixed together, will abide for you. I will not always be a good person, or a good mother, but I will try. I will try and keep on trying for you, for thrice three hundred years, until the woman from the south marries the man from the north. Until our gods change shape. I will keep trying.'

And I know that it would have been a lie, and that they would not have heard me in a way that would have eased things. But I think there is value in words leaving a mouth. In good intentions. In not holding feelings in like thick black smoke until they char the inside of your ribcage and slowly bright orange embers flicker and begin to flame. Until your fury makes you incandescent.

There was so little good in me to even turn to ash. And that day, with the sun bright in the sky and the white walls and soft green grass of Sídh Finnachadh looking as serene and lovely as a swan upon a lake, I left my room, and I washed my face, my body. And I asked for a chariot to be brought to me. And I went in search of Fionnuala and Aodh and Fiachra and Conn. That I might ask them to accompany me to Sídh Femuin, to visit their grandfather.

SCÉAL

And when the chariot passed Loch Dairbhreach, Aífe asked the charioteer to stop for a while, that the children might swim in the water. And, though Fionnuala was hesitant to do so, she followed her three brothers in to the shining waters of the lake. And while they were swimming, Aífe ordered the charioteer to slay the Children of Lir. And when he refused, she drew forth a sword of her own to do it, but her womanhood and natural cowardice kept her from doing so, and so instead she produced a wand and called forth a spell upon the innocent Children of Lir, which turned them into four shining swans, and gave them no way to return to their natural forms or to break the spell until nine hundred years had passed. Three hundred on Loch Dairbhreach, another three hundred on the Straits of Moyle and three hundred more again on Iorrus Domnann and Inis Gluaire. The swans turned towards her and, feeling some remorse, Aífe granted them the power of speech and song before she went on her way to the castle of her foster-father.

MUIN

I hurt them badly I did not protect your children, Áebh

Loch Dairbhreach is not as it once was, though it is still lovely. I see it from above now, rather than from the ground. The shining waters and the lush green fields. Protective mounds of stones. It was particularly beautiful that day and, had I not been bent upon my task, I would have been tempted to have a dip myself. Perhaps I should have done, washed myself clean of all my sins, and taken the children to collect berries until our stomachs were full and our mouths ran red with juice.

The Children of Lir, with various levels of enthusiasm, made their cautious way in to the water, but once inside the lake, their moods lifted. They had their father's affinity for water, and loved to be in it. Their white-blond heads soon bobbed up and down beneath the waves and I looked at them and felt such a keen sense of hatred. I do not understand what so enraged me about them. It may have simply been that they had forgotten I was there and found joy in doing so. That would have been enough, perhaps, to do it. They looked so happy to be in their own skins, and I wanted desperately to take that from them, to mar and break and ruin something good. And they were good. It is so simple, to be happy in the sunshine, in the water. Life wasn't simple, though, and I felt like a cloud about to burst. Something terrible was about to happen. Breathing in the air and lake and leaves, I made my move.

I turned to the charioteer, Liath, my attendant, Seona, and the warrior, Broc, and tilted my head in a manner that had proven pleasing in the past. I smiled, and I could see the hesitancy on their faces. And I did not ask them to kill the Children of Lir, though I intended to harm those children if I lived.

Instead, I drew a sword and presented the hilt of it towards them. My hands wrapped around the blade, and I could see the distaste on their faces as the blood pooled on it. It was an old sword, it had been Dechtaire's once, and it was hungry. It had not been fed in quite some time. My eyes met the charioteer's first, as he was the strongest and the most obedient. And I asked him to slay me, for fear of what I'd do if he did not.

He shook his head and turned his face away, and I could see the shame he felt for me in the low slope of his shoulders. I turned to Seona next, knowing her child was sick, offered her all kinds of treasures, access to the magical healing apples that had come from across the waves at great cost. And I could see many feelings flutter across her face. She tried to approach me and I gripped the blade more tightly. It cut deep. It was as though I were a missing beast who had been hurt, who must be approached gently. Had she produced a little cut of meat to tempt me to her, I would not have been surprised and I hated that it almost worked on me, those wide eyes, that urging me to give in and give up.

Broc simply grabbed the sword from me and wiped it on the grass. I think, perhaps, if we had been alone, he might have done it. He really didn't like me. Not very many people did by then. I had been cruel at times, and very difficult. The suddenness of his movement shook something loose in me, convinced me of the rightness of my actions. No-one understood what had been taken from me, always, always. They saw that I was hurt and kept on taking. What little hope I had of visiting my family, my sister, in the Otherworld was gone. I felt warmth behind my eyes and breathed the tears back inside me. I could have melted into nothing then, gone back to the *sídh*, let Lir do what he would until death found me. But I refused. And so it was the worse for me, and all around me.

I saw Fionnuala's head bob through the water. She was swimming closer to the shore. I clapped my hands and pressed them to the ground so deeply that I felt the earth itself enter my veins, flow through me. We were one. In that moment I became a facet of the goddess. A hungry, angry elemental thing. I could have remade the world itself in my image, I could have shoved the mountains back inside the earth and raised the lakes to claim the dwellings near them. The knowledge of all that had been, and all that would be, flowed through me then. And I could have endured there for ever, perhaps changing shape into a tree or stone. Something older, stronger than a person, even one of the Tuatha Dé Danann. We were not the same as the Invaders. We were more beautiful, more powerful. More difficult to kill. But we had eyes and mouths and bones and hearts, and it was my own beating heart that drew me back to where I was then. When I opened my eyes, day had turned into night and the children were still there inside the water. I did not look for Liath, Seona or Broc. They were nearby, but that was immaterial. They could have no more intervened than a fly could prevent dogs' jaws from clamping down on a delicious cut of meat. Everyone seemed smaller and lesser than myself, they didn't matter. Only their interactions with me gave them meaning and there it stopped. I was myself but that was someone else and she was glorious.

My hair was streaming around my face in three separate locks, and my green cloak was flapping like the dark wings of a bird. My feet had risen above the moist suck of the earth. And I looked upon the Children of Lir, as a cat looks upon a mouse when she has time. And I decided to play with them, as Lir had played with me.

Ferns and flowering herbs bordered the lake, and I could sense them moving, filtering what they needed from the sharp air. Sucking in a little bit of power. Everything in this hard world is hungry. And only sometimes do we get to feast. I stretched out my hand, and a thin wand, carved from the smooth bones of Diangalach, slid out of my robes and down my wrist. It felt, as it must have done when it lived in his flesh. Warm and smooth and potent.

I saw understanding dawn in Fionnuala's eyes. And I held the wand above my head and drew the power of the air into it. And then I sank it into the waters of the lake and drew on those as well. I did not stick it deep inside the earth. The Children of Lir were no longer welcome there. And my tongue and throat moved in ancient ways, in ways that they had spoken before speech, and I unmade the bodies of the Children of Lir, unwrapped their hair and skin from round their bones and wove those bones like witches into another shape. I stretched their necks long and pressed their feet flat, and I gave them the waters of the lake inside their hearts and a longing for the cold rush of air beneath their wings.

In the story, it says I struck them, and they turned into four white swans. This is inaccurate. What I did involved unwinding and remaking. Weaving and warping. It hurt them deeply and it hurt my soul as well to do it. But I was full of resolve, and when I felt my heart soften, I would bite down hard on my own tongue as I had often done in bed with their father as he tried to get sons on me while I was in a dark and lonely place. By the end, my teeth were red with blood and I could taste myself inside myself.

My hair was plastered with sweat to my face and my garments also dripped with it. And the Children of Lir sat elegantly upon the water, barely more than cygnets, with dirt-brown feathers mixing through the white, and two even younger cygnets, soft with down. All with small, black, unreadable eyes. And it was their youth, I suppose, the fragility of them, that allowed the wave of my anger to break on the shore. I plummeted down to the ground with an inelegant thunk that sent a shiver of pain from ankle through to thigh, and I limped towards the three small cobs and one slightly larger pen that had been made of the same stuff as me that very morning. The wand fell from my hand as I approached them.

I reached my hand out, and the Children of Lir, who should have recoiled from me, instead came closer. Their black-lined beaks opened and shut, and the noises escaping from their mouths were high and harsh. I moved toward them, and one of them, a cob, perhaps my Aodh, pressed his little head into the palm of my hand. I could feel the eight black eyes staring at me, pleading, bright as blackberries.

Change us back!

My hand reached for the wand. It wasn't there. The blood rushed to my head and I could feel a mounting sense of panic. I scrabbled in the mud to no avail. It was gone. I never again found it.

They were so small. They were my sister's babes. I felt that suddenly and forcefully inside my heart. I had taken them from their home, and they would be untethered now, and it wasn't their fault that I was the way I was.

The transformation was complete, and could not be undone, but I searched my power for some small way to ease their burden, reason fighting anger, neither winning. I gave them speech and reason. I wanted to give them places to belong to. Homes to make. And perhaps I wasn't thinking clearly, or perhaps some of the goddess was left in me, for the words I spoke did not feel like my words. I listened to myself give them three hundred years here, at this kind lake, to get used to who and what they were now. I gave them three hundred years on the Straits of Moyle, that they might leave their father lonely and know the cruel power of the seas, the salt, the lash, the flicker of lightning and the roar of thunder. That they might come out the other side, resilient. I gave them three hundred years between Iorrus Domnann and Inis Gluaire, that they might have an island to call home. I gave them their voices, that they might condemn me, and I gave them song so beautiful and powerful that it would cast a spell on all who heard it and ward off any threat with ears to hear. I gave them hope, that their sentence would be over when the world was a different sort of place and my power weaker, when the man from the north would listen to the woman from the south and do her bidding. And, moved by their compassion, which faded once their senses returned, I gave them my rage, to use against me. That they might hate me and want to survive and band together in spite of what I'd done to them, to show me that they could. That I had changed nothing in their love for each other. That they were still a family. Four dappled half-grown things pretending strength. Fionnuala flapped her wings and reared her head and hissed, and Fiachra and Conn sheltered under her grey-white wings, while Aodh crouched before her submissively.

She was the first to speak from this new throat.

'Aífe,' she said, and her new shape deepened her voice, added a resonance to it, that so resembled the way her mother spoke. It shook me.

'Aífe,' she said again. I shrank from her, and a great shame came over me, and a great desire to never look upon the faces of the children of Aébh, on the shapes that I had made from them again.

I rested my two hands in the lake and my two feet on the earth and sought my power.

It was very weak, and I could use no more of it. But it was there. What I had done had diminished me, but not extinguished me. I thought of all the slaughter Bodhbh had done, even before this wicked time of war, and Lir besides. I thought of the scheming and the cruelty of the people around me, and I tried to find a sort of innocence for myself among their guilts.

It was not a noble impulse, but I am not a noble sort of creature. I never was. Oillill of Aran should have held my head beneath the waves when I was born and kept me from my purpose in this world, which seemed to be in hurting other people. In disappointing them. In revenging myself upon innocents, who cannot help their lineage.

What I had done to them, to Aébh's four children, was not precisely kin-slaying, but it was a kind of slaughter anyway, of the future they had envisioned for themselves, a reshaping of it into something very different and undoubtedly more lonely. At least, I mused, I had left them with each other. And some of my anger to heat them through the storms and cold, long nights when their soft wings would ache with this harsh world.

The druidic mist I had called down abated and lifted, and the three who'd watched it happen blinked and stared at me, as though I had come down from out of the sky. Not a word was spoken on the way to my father's fortress by any one of our number. We rode grimly together. And I had no fear but that they would hold their tongues. This crime was mine to admit to, and though our people knew of the power and potential of magic, this story, in the time before these tales of wicked stepmothers and all that they were capable of, was so far-fetched that, even when later on it came from my own mouth, it needed to be proven with something more than words. The swans, bound to remain on the lake for centuries to come, were necessary.

I scrolled through my brain for what to tell Bodhbh the Red.

SCÉAL

And Aífe arrived at the palace of Bodhbh Dearg, and there was a fine welcome for her there. And her foster-father asked her why she had come alone, without the Children of Lir by her side. The deceitful Aífe told him that Lir had not permitted his sons and daughter to accompany her, as he had no liking for Bodhbh the Red and was plotting against him.

Wise Bodhbh wondered at this changing story and, sensing lies, sent his messengers north to Sídh Finnachadh to confirm his foster-daughter's tale.

HUATH

I deserve

no shelter from sharp teeth

When my people, the Tuatha Dé Danann, arrived in Ireland, some say we came through the air, in a great mist. They say we left a glorious homeland behind us and that our treasures – the Spear of Victory, the Stone of Destiny, the Sword of Light and the Cauldron of Plenty – were from this place, this home before our home.

But when we retreated, as we did in the wake of the Invaders, we withdrew slowly into the earth and the deep water, the dark and sacred spaces in the world. We took our magic with us. I say 'we', though at this stage, I was but an observer, outside of the tribe. No-one ventured back into the air. Caer and her lover, Aengus Óg, had mastery over it, and Aengus showed a love and respect for all the creatures of the air in particular. But birds, though they journey through it, return at night to nest in trees, on roofs. We all need somewhere we can rest our head.

Air and fire are necessary sometimes, but earth and water, those two. Those are our essence. They were *mine*. The closest thing I had to home, my power grew from them and tethered me to the world. Because of this, and because of the punishment I have experienced, I will say this. I do not think the air was ever our home. Perhaps we journeyed on it as a means to an end. Perhaps we were cast out and would not admit it in our songs and stories, not even to ourselves.

I have had a lot of time to think.

When the chariot stopped, they let me out. I looked at the three of them, their faces. And hissed, 'Be gone from here.'

They ran, as though from a wolf or a wild boar, and I was glad of it. The horror of what had happened was written on their skin in such a way that it would not escape Bodhbh's notice. I had thought that, upon the way, I would compose myself, concoct a tale that would make sense of everything.

I had not done that.

I had no idea what I would do.

The guardian of the door did not nod his head as I approached, and I was uncertain if I would be welcome. My face. My eyes. The dishevelled nature of my clothing, hair. The dirt on me, the muck of lake and wetland. I raised myself to my full height and eyed him imperiously. I was the foster-daughter of a king. I was the wife of Lir. And most importantly I was myself. I could unmake him with a wave of my hand and it would not be the worst thing I had done that day.

He shrank a little and then I saw Ailbhe run towards me. Her feet fast and quiet against the earth. A warrior knows the value of silence. Seeing her, my bravado left me, and I felt my face begin to crack like an egg. I was fiercely drawn into my sister's embrace.

Her cloak smelled of sweat and forest dirt and the warm skin that had been beside me as I slept until I left this place to marry

Lir. The closest thing to home I'd ever known. And the safety of that undid me utterly. Tears crowded in my eyes. Not the crystal tears of a deceitful woman, but the ugly tears of a desperate one. Without a word, Ailbhe swept me away from the fortress and down the hill, half-carrying me, as I bent double, wailing as deeply and powerfully as a woman in the throes of birthing. When we could no longer see the stone of the *sidh* my breath relented a little. She said nothing, but her arms kept my two feet on the ground, fixed me in this world. I became aware of the sensations in my body. The wet slap of the cloak against my skin. We kept on moving, past the hill where we had sat with Aébh and watched her babies play, we walked again, we kept on walking, through the trees. I knew where we were going. We did not have to speak. A safe, small space. A little cave that we had played in as children, pretending that it was our own home that we came from. We would take turns being our mother and our father and then ourselves. The game just involved the daughter asking questions and finding answers. They varied according to who was being who, and they were closer, I knew even then, to the truths we wanted than to the truths that were.

We sat, two sisters on an earth- and leaf-strewn floor. I could hear the whisper of the breeze through the leaves on the trees, and I thought of all the whispering there would be until it reached his ears.

What I had done.

I couldn't look at it.

It was too much.

'Aífe,' she said, her voice reaching through the silence that stretched between us. Her hair, bright as an ember, soft as a leaf, was pulled back from her face. And I kept thinking, *If she knew. If she knew the things that I have done. Who am I now? Have I put her in danger?* And I looked at my two hands and at her face. I had. I had. As surely as if I had wrapped them round her neck and throttled the life out of her myself. I felt like I was moving far away. Very far from where and who I was and looking down upon myself from a great height, with old and tired eyes that had seen much and didn't care to speak.

She said my name again, 'Aífe'. As though it were a chain around my neck to draw me out of myself and toward her. As though there were a name for what I am. She put her strong hand on my back, and I saw the sword at her waist and swallowed.

She might kill me for this, I remember thinking.

And I might deserve it.

The wind cut through the hawthorn trees and the sky was brightening again. I looked at my feet, still thick with river mud. The dirt of the lake clung to me.

My sister held me.

And I thought, not of myself, but of another person. Had this impulse arrived earlier in my tale, it would have been better for all concerned. But the world is not our servant and moves not for us but in spite of us.

My panic cut the silence as inelegantly as a plough. I breathed in the night inside my lungs. I held it there. I did that once again until the hum of it slowed down in me. I knew, of course, that time was of the essence. But I needed the next thing I said to be the thing that helped instead of hurt. To persuade her of a course of action that I did not think would sit well with her duty or her valour.

'Ailbhe,' I said, and though it was dark I could make out the features of her face, clear as that man could that had the cat's eye, 'you need to leave.'

She made a contemptuous noise.

'No,' I said. 'No, really. Not for your own sake, but for mine. I have ... I have done something wrong. Something terribly wrong. And when Bodhbh finds out, he will kill all belonging to me.'

I looked at her. 'You know him. You can see this.'

This time my sister did not say my name, and her hands stilled on my back as I began my story. I had the chariot. I had the horses. I had some gold, bracelets, earrings, rings. The trappings of a noblewoman. I took them as I spoke and I wrapped them in a piece torn from my cloak.

'I deserve everything that's coming to me, sister. But you do not. This could get you across the sea, to Alban. You could train with the warrior woman there.'

'Scathach,' she breathed.

'Yes,' I said, 'she will take you on if you are good enough. And you are good enough.'

'What you did ...' she said.

'I hurt Aébh's children. I used my power to twist and warp their shape as my own self has twisted and warped inside me these past years. I am nothing good now. No good will come of me. But you –' I grasped my fingers, tight as snares around her wrist. 'Your future is unwritten. I did not protect them, and I could have. Let me protect you. It is the only hope that I have left to me.'

Her face was blurry through the sting of tears. I had lake muck in my nail beds as well and it had entered my eyes and it was blinding, stinging. I could not read her.

'What you did,' she said again, and her voice was harsh, 'cannot go unpunished.'

'I know that much. Believe me that I will be. I will tell Bodhbh what I have done, and he will tell Lir and between the two of them, they will find a price for me to pay. But you are blameless in this, Ailbhe – and I want more for you than I will get. Our parents do not live. You are the last of our line. You could go abroad, take a new name, a new life. A warrior who only serves herself.'

I touched her wrist and closed my eyes. It is hard to read a person's future. Hope gets in the way. The earth beneath my feet, my sister's pulse. Then ... something.

'The smell of salt and sand. A mountain and a fire. A little hero. He will end in blood but you will live.'

'I don't want to have no-one,' Ailbhe said.

'You will have yourself. And she is powerful,' I told her, making my red eyes as wide and fierce as I could. 'I see more years. Some years, at least.'

'Where are the children now?' she asked of me, and I told her. She stood up and began gathering her things.

'I will go to them and beg forgiveness for your crimes. We will not meet again, sister. I wish that you had found it easier to be in the world. I wish that your pain had not curled out like a whip to lash at others. I wish we could have been old together and found our way to a boat ... and back to the island.'

'You could see it again,' I said to her.

She nodded. 'I cannot tell if this is cowardly or not. It feels that way.'

'It's what I want. Please. Give me this small flame.'

I laid my hands on her and pushed with the dregs of my power, to guide her way through the dark, that the woods might protect her and the seas not claim her. There was little left inside me after that, but it felt like a small good thing to do, in the wake of the evil I had wrought.

And when I walked back towards Sídh Femuin, to await our foster-father's judgement, my sister had left with everything I'd brought and more besides. And the old man knew full well that something was amiss. He didn't miss a trick. He never had.

'Where is your sister?' he asked me.

'I do not know,' I said, and my eyes were wild enough and my cloak that torn that he decided not to pursue it, and instead took my face in his hands, in a gesture that would have been fatherly if I could not feel the joints of his fingers pressing hard against my cheekbones, the fleshy part of his palm making my lips purse inelegantly. His thumbs were just beneath my eye sockets, and it would only take a very little for them to delve inside, to pulse and gouge.

'You look upset,' he said, and pulled me to his chest and stroked my hair. I could hear the beating of his heart and feel the hard muscle against my body. The threat of him.

'I am well, father,' I said. 'Just tired, after all the travelling.'

'And the children?' he asked. 'They are not with you.'

'No,' I said to him. 'Not any more.'

And, in spite of the shame that flowed through me already at this deed that I had done, there was a moment when I felt triumphant, that I had hurt something that he held dear. That I could surprise and horrify this man. That I could crack his implacable face in two. He had no idea of the power I wielded. The threat that I could pose. And I wondered, if, when my reserves of strength had been replenished, perhaps there would be a way. A use for me. Once he saw my potential.

But that was stupid of me. And I gave it but a moment. I had angered Lir, a rival who had reason to mis-like Bodhbh already. I had hurt the grandchildren he loved. I had been unruly, disobedient. I had been violent in an unsanctioned manner, and used powers that he had not allowed me to have. My vengeance was not the sort that warriors admired, that people sang about. It was a lowly sort, and he would be ashamed of me, disgusted.

My fury curled within me again.

It had brought me back in to the world.

And though I feared and hated what it had led to, I was grateful.

I could taste the smoke on the air, smell the rushes on the floor. Hear the sounds of other people's feet. All of it was going in to me. I was so far from numb. I could feel everything.

'Where are the children, Aífe?' Bodhbh said.

And I knew that he knew that I had done something to them.

And I knew that he knew that I knew.

But this dance had steps, and we both knew them. And every moment that I drew them out was a moment Ailbhe might have need of soon. An instant in which to hear the crunch of feet, the soft threat of a quietly drawn sword. And my sister was fierce, and she was strong. A beat could be enough to doom her foes.

'They are occupied,' I said. 'I left them amusing themselves together. They did not care to come with me, even to visit you. It is no secret I have not been well.'

'Lir informed me,' he said, and the terse note in his voice said a multitude of unflattering things.

I swallowed and I stared at the centre of his beard, the parting where the forks of hair began. It was paler than the rest of his skin. And I thought of the two great wings of a swan. The power in them. They are what swans use when they attack. I felt a threat coming towards me on the air. From the four of them, the children I had hurt.

'I am more myself than I was,' I told him, and there was no lie in that. 'I feel stronger.' And there was truth to that too. I chose my words very carefully.

'I hope to be the wife that Lir deserves.'

His mouth crooked, in something between a smile and a grimace. 'I'm glad to hear that, child.'

I rose to my full height, which was shorter than him, and pushed myself up further through the air, until our eyes met, and I saw the flash of surprise in his. I stayed there, just a little show of power. A flex of it. My cloak was long enough to trail the ground; if you had not registered how tall I was before, you wouldn't even notice.

I don't even know why I did it really, there was so little power left in me that I could feel the drain of holding my place. I lowered myself to the ground slowly, and with a satisfied sigh. I wanted him to see that I could do things. That there was value in the skill I had. And it was futile. Weak, even. It showed him, I think, the game that I had played. At least a little.

When Bodhbh played *ficheall*, he saw the whole game out before him move by move, as surely as a druid reads the entrails of a beast. We strike at each other to gauge who we might be and who we are.

My foster-father stepped away from me.

'Aífe,' he said, 'what have you done?'

'Lir should be arriving soon,' I told him. 'And maybe he will tell you himself. The story of the fine wife that you gave him. And how she repaid his love.'

'Leave the room,' Bodhbh said, 'all of you. Even my Nine.'

I could see his eyes scanning my face as they left, looking for a hint of what had happened. It had to be bad, bad enough to anger Lir. But what could it be?

And, though he was very good at seeing all the moves that lay ahead, it is a rare daughter who turns her husband's children into magical swans. It seems like the sort of thing a reasonable person could see the pitfalls of.

I had lost my reason, though, and found my fury. It was curled in the core of me now, like a contented cat that had lapped cream. I stretched and yawned, and did not put my hand upon my mouth. I showed that man my teeth. Let him count them. My wounds were not white. I had suffered for what strength I had, and as I looked at him, I had the strangest sense of kinship; if I had done a bad thing, so had he. Bodhbh's hands were dark with well-remembered gore.

I have had a lot of time to think. And I have told myself this story, the one that I am telling you right now, time and time again. And I never come out perfect. No-one does. The closest, perhaps, is Aébh in men's eyes, Ailbhe to my eyes. My small bright hope.

'What did you do?' my foster-father asked me, and his voice was the voice that he uses for men he considers rivals.

'My husband,' I said, rolling the word around my tongue with just the right level of contempt, 'has not been best pleased with me, father. Do you think that he would entrust his children, who he professes to love more than anything in the world, to one such as I, who has so disappointed him?'

Bodhbh looked at me and stroked one of the forks of his ridiculous beard.

'I have lost much. My home. My sister. The place I knew the best. My heart. My hope. My wits. I have had a surfeit of loss, King Bodhbh.'

'To live in this world is to lose things, Aífe,' he said, and his voice was stern, but also something else.

'But what of winning?'

'Many people never do,' he said, and his face was serious. 'If everyone were a king, a crown would be no great prize. If everyone were a champion, no squabbles would erupt over the champion's portion. Greatness is rare. And it is not easily won or easily maintained. I do not rule this land of ours lightly, but I do rule it well. Everyone makes sacrifices, daughter. Everyone.' His words were straight and pointed, and I found myself wondering what it would have been like if he had spoken to me in this way before. As though I were his equal. Which I both was and wasn't. The land had welcomed him, had chosen him. I looked him in the eye and named my pain. Short words for deepest hurts.

'He did not love me.'

He closed his eyes and opened them again.

'Oh, Aífe,' he said, 'all of that for this. Love is not so very much. It will not keep bread in your mouth and cloth on your back. Lir could have been a step to something better. If only you had learned to bide your time.'

'I didn't want something better,' I told him. 'It was only something that was my own I wanted. And it was foolish to keep wanting for things to change, to be better for me or kinder to me, but I couldn't help it, and every thing I'd ever wanted and not got became another stone in a wall, until I couldn't see over it. And I needed a way out of where I found myself, a way out of feeling wrong and helpless and alone, so I reached inside myself and found an anger there that I could use.'

'Anger has a lot to teach a person. But distance makes it easier to wield. Child, what could this power do, exactly?' he asked, and there was a weariness in his eyes, a resignation. I thought of how old he must be now. The Dagda's son.

'I have learned not to build. Building is hopeful work. I have learned not to create. Creation is too often forced on women.'

I thought of my back against the dirt of the floor in that small room and Lir's impatient breath. I rubbed my shoulder and felt the indignity of that again, the skin rubbed raw and the eyes unmet. A flicker of my rage pulsed. Just a little hint. It was still there. I knew it and it knew me and we were entwined, the two of us together. The earth beneath my feet and the water that ran, fresh and sparkling, beneath it.

'What does your power do, if not create things?' he asked me. 'Does it divine our fate, or change the course?'

'It destroys,' I told him. 'I have a talent for destruction, foster-father. My hands are dark with the gore of what I have done. I took those children, and I destroyed them. They are children no more. They are wild creatures, with wild hearts and long white throats that they may sing their pain in to the evening. Lir will approach soon, and he will tell you this. That, in a fit of evil, I turned his children in to swans.'

Bodhbh looked at me, and his face twisted into something unfamiliar. I thought, at first, that it was disgust. To hurt a child was horror to our people. It was not like now, where children are alternately treasured and neglected. They were rare and precious things to us. And I had thought that he had love for those children, for what they meant, an alliance made, a foe turned friend, but also for themselves, their merry faces and their little ways. The thirst that children have for love and laughter.

But no, my foster-father barked with laughter.

'He won't like that,' he said. 'Oh, he'll *hate* that.'

I had not seen his real face before, perhaps. And there it was and I was suddenly unsure of myself. Of the way I saw the world. Bodhbh's pleasure in what I had done was clear. I had not realised the enmity that was between them still. He hid it well.

'I gave you to him to vex him, and you vexed him. But even I could not have predicted this.'

'Lir will say that I have lost my wits, and perhaps I have. Perhaps I am a dark, unpleasant creature. But I am my own creature. I am mine, my feet on the earth and the water in my soul and fire in my heart. And when all is taken from me, I will still have my anger and my pain and they will feed me.'

'Was it so very bad to be our daughter?' he asked me.

'I would not know,' I said.

'You are a child. A selfish, selfish child,' he said and shook his head. 'Were your father not already dead, he would be killed for this, your mother too. When Lir arrives, I am going to be surprised and shocked by what you've done, and I will punish you in ways you cannot comprehend. Ways I will have to think on. But know this, I am not punishing you for what you did to your sister's children. I am punishing you for disobeying me. You shirked your duty and you have disgraced yourself, your name and your line. You think that you have power? I am the son of a god.'

He raised his hands and let a fraction of what he could do run through me, turn my bones to mercury. I collapsed on the floor.

'True power means that I almost never use my magic. I do not have to hurt you, Aífe. I could have you killed, or shunned, or banished. I could give you as a prize to any number of mercenaries. I could shut you up inside the belly of a freshly slaughtered mare, or bury you alive. There are so many things that I could do with a snap of my fingers, but I want this to last. And what a pleasure, to show you and everybody else what happens when people who do not deserve power try to use it, for what? You desired to anger Lir with your cruelty? I will shake the very world with mine. And I am king, so people will remember it as justice. Now, sit and wait for what will come to pass.'

He swept his hand across the throne room and I took small steps into the corner where I sat calmly with my hands folded in my lap, lips pressed together, eyes downcast. A fly crawled across my face and I could not raise my hand or twitch my skin to brush it off. It crept in to the corner of my eye.

'Good girl,' said Bodhbh, and called his Nine back in.

SCÉAL

When Bodhbh's people arrived at Sídh Finnachadh, they found Lir without his children. And they found the lie in Aífe's story, and Lir was heart-sore and much worried, for he knew that some devilment had been done on his poor children. He made haste to Sídh Femuin to question her himself. And on the way, he stopped, as was his custom, at Loch Dairbhreach, to give the horses a break. And there he encountered the four enchanted swans, who informed him of Aífe's villainy. Upon learning that there was no relief for them from her terrible curse, Lir and his people raised three great shouts of grief, and tears came to the eyes of all who heard them, though they knew not why.

Lir arrived at the home of Bodhbh the Red and informed him of the malign and brazen thing his foster-daughter had done, and Bodhbh was shocked indeed at the depth of her villainy. He asked her what punishment she would fear the most, and she answered, 'To be turned into a demon of the air.'

Bodhbh struck her with his druidical wand, and Aífe was changed into a demon of the air, a horrible creature. Bodhbh commanded her to stay that way for ever, shunned, despised and knowing no relief. 'Nine hundred years will pass for the Children of Lir,' said Bodhbh. 'But time will never stop for you: your treachery has condemned you for ever.'

And Aífe flew away. She's flying still.

STRAIF

a witch

I am a wicked woman in a story I am

a scream

long

in throats

white

It took a while for Bodhbh's messengers to reach Lir, and a while again for Lir to reach me. I sat, still and obedient, all the while. Eyes moving, lungs filling with air, but there was no freedom for me. The earth beneath my feet did not connect with me. And it was not the same as the terrible void I had experienced. I had my wits about me, but I could not use them. I had energy, but I was restrained, as surely as a hound with a chain around his neck.

I would try to use my power every now and then, to push at the edges of my body. To explore. To see if there could be a way to loose the bonds, to find a way to free myself. To run. A small amount at first, and then as I became more afraid of what was coming, I gave it everything, to no avail.

I know that if I were any sort of person, I should have faced my punishment head on, but that became less easy as time passed and the anticipation of what exactly would happen to me began to build. I had nothing else to think about but what was coming. I stood when he made my body stand. I smiled and clapped at the music, and the poetry, because the edges of my mouth were pushed up tightly and my hands forced together.

Puppets were not commonplace back then, so there was no word I knew for what he had made of me. He was the son of a god, and I was the daughter of a man and woman I could not recall. I did not dare to let my mind flicker to Ailbhe, as I felt he was party to all my thoughts. Whenever I tried to so much as wiggle a toe I felt his power clench around my body. And so I played the part he had me play, the wolf in sheep's clothing, and waited for my doom to come.

And come it did.

Lir entered the fort and went for me. His hands wrapped around my short pink throat. I felt Bodhbh's hold on me relax, and I tried to grab his wrists, to meet his eyes. This man had lain with me, had called me precious. All that was left in him was hate and rage.

'Unhand her,' said Bodhbh with a sweep of his hand.

Lir did not comply.

Bodhbh nodded his head at the Nine, and they tore him from me. I crouched on the floor like a woman in childbirth, gasping and retching. Lir struggled and fought against the Nine, but they had him fast. His eyes never left my face. I climbed to my feet and smoothed down my dress. My death was coming. I could almost taste it.

They would not let me leave this place again.

I stood, trying to hold my head regally upon the bruised mess of my neck. My voice could barely work.

'Lir,' I said, and it was low and rasping. It could have meant a number of things to him. Defiance or contrition. I wasn't sure what it even meant to me, exactly. Why I said his name. Why, if I could have, I would have reached out and touched his angry face. He could not help it, being who he was. And I would soon have no need of him, or want for him. It would be over.

Many men have killed their wives over the years, and in many different fashions. They poison them, they hold their heads underneath the water, they take a knife to them or their two strong hands. They neglect them, or pay them too much attention. They become jealous, or they do not care. They take other lovers, and share with them diseases of the flesh. They control their possessions, and make them ask for every little thing. They chide them, day by day, until the things they've said take root and become a sort of truth that eats away at what they were before. So very many women torn in to shreds.

And, when something dreadful comes to pass, then we tell the stories of these men. How gentle they were, how polite. How clear and calm their brows. What good fathers they were. How much they did for those around them. What a surprise! What a surprise it was. As if it were a foreign thing indeed, a brave new notion for the people to have more than one face, or to hurt those closest to them badly. As if there were no clear idea who the wronged party might have been. I don't mean to ally myself with wronged parties here. Though there were ways in which I had been wronged. I did what I did and I suffer the weight of it, but I wonder, if my vision had come to pass and Lir had killed me, would people be too busy forgiving him to remember who I was?

Distasteful stories make us seek new stories. And stories are powerful things indeed. As I was about to find out.

Lir looked at Bodhbh. 'She has taken my children from me, Bodhbh. And turned them into …'

He did not call him 'King'.

Bodhbh noticed that. I saw him notice that.

Oh, Lir, I thought, *you do yourself no favours.*

And I smiled. For whatever hurt Bodhbh had in store for me, and it was coming, I could feel it coming, he had something else in mind for Lir. The bullish look upon my husband's face was priceless. I felt for him and hated him at the same time, and it was like a cloth that a sword had been wiped clean on. My stupid hopes, and how they had been dashed.

It had never been about me, or even Aébh.

It was these two men, circling each other. Vying for dominance.

One a born leader, a fierce warrior.

One the son of a god.

'All except my Nine, leave the room,' Bodhbh said. 'Lir and Aífe, remain with me. Let us find the truth of this.'

Lir nodded, and the Nine stepped away from him. They were Nine again, I noticed. Ailbhe had been replaced already. They didn't move too far away. I could see the tension in his muscles, the clench of his fists. The little flecks of spittle in the corners of his mouth. His pupils had been so wide when he came at me, like the eyes of a cat studying its prey. I wondered if he would take my life before Bodhbh had the chance to mete out whatever punishment he had in store. And I hoped he wouldn't. I knew whatever faced me would be difficult, but my pride would not allow me to wish for a swift death at the hands of this man who had taught me so much about love and hate and how intertwined they are, like braids of hair.

The room was quieter now. I could hear the shuffle and breath of the men around me, and the air was thick with a promise or a threat. I tried to connect to the earth beneath me, and the water in it, nourishing the life within. *Goddess, give me the strength to accept my punishment. Give me a sense of peace as I cross over to the Otherworld. Let me find my family. Let me find Aébh, and beg her for forgiveness. Let me cross paths with Dechtaire and Smól. Let me find my mother and my father. And let us sit together, beside one another, each one knowing who the others are, that the ocean flows through our veins. That we come from the same place. That we are in the same place.*

I closed my eyes and breathed. And that image found me. And the goddess gave me their faces, clear and just as Dechtaire and Smól had told us, but with more depth, with little marks and flaws that people have. Our mother had the furrow Ailbhe had between her eyebrows. There was so much to notice in a short space of time. We are all different people to different people. Bodhbh and Lir were discussing my treachery. Counting every thorn on my branches. Deciding what to do. I let their words run over me like water. Soon, I thought. Soon I would be safe. They could not touch me. And maybe, in the next life, I could be a salmon or a hare. A wild and flickering thing, living by instinct, tethered only to elements and the needs of my small body. I was so sure that I could taste my death.

I remember thinking, *If I get through the hours, or days, or weeks that Bodhbh has planned, then at the end, there will be something close to peace for me.* A peace I hadn't found in this life.

I thought that I had some idea of what was coming.

I had none.

I had, in spite of my upbringing, in spite of our conversations and in spite of my own keen wits, underestimated what my foster-father was capable of.

I had been broken once and had mended myself, piece by aching piece. I felt the scars on me. The lingering pain and guilt and, yes, the anger too. It hadn't left me, it still lay in wait.

I thought I knew what suffering entailed.

I'd no idea.

Bodhbh and Lir stared at me, and Bodhbh waved his hands. The Nine were upon me quickly and efficiently. I was pulled to my feet and forced to my knees in front of them.

Bodhbh's voice was deep and resonant, like a druid casting a spell.

'Call in the druids and the poets,' he said. 'I would have them see this wretch's fate'

And so they were brought in, the creators and custodians of our collective memory. My eyes flickered from the central stone in front of me to the feet collecting around me.

'This wilful woman has wrought a great evil upon our dear friend Lir,' Bodhbh pronounced, 'and will suffer in proportion to her crimes. The Children of Lir have had their bodies taken from them, their futures stolen and reshaped beyond comprehension through unnatural scheming and witchery. Aífe's spite and villainy have taken something that cannot be replaced from this noble chieftain. And as their grandfather, and as his king, I would right that wrong, in whatever way I can.'

The room was silent. Everyone was holding in their breath for what approached.

Bodhbh produced a wand from the folds of his cloak.

'This wand was given to me by my father. It was carved from a blackthorn of great power, and he imbued it with magic of his own. I have not used it in a hundred years.'

Lir stood behind Bodhbh, his face resolute, his eyes on me. I could see how badly he desired to be the one to hurt me, and how deeply he hungered for that hurt.

I swallowed. My throat was very dry and very sore. My robes had ridden up and my knees were bare against the floor. Blood trickled from one of my nostrils, but my hands were pinioned at my sides and the back of my head was held fast. I could neither wipe the blood nor tilt my head back to stem the flow.

Bodhbh told my story. The story you have heard, of a wise king and a good man and three daughters, one perfect, one evil and one inconsequential. Of a betrayal, born of jealousy and the need for vengeance. Of a woman enslaved to her worst qualities, and the cruelty she had wrought on innocent children and the father who loved them above all. And there was truth in it, but not the full truth either. And I knew, as his mouth moved and their heads nodded slowly, and their voices gasped and murmured at certain parts, that this was how I would be remembered.

He would reshape what I had done as surely as I had warped those children in to swans. But while I had a modicum of mercy, he had none. He would leave me ugly and alone. Shunned by all, remembered only as a rotten thing.

It was hard to hear. Particularly the truth in it. It stung my pride, this tearing at the flesh of who I had been and rearranging the pieces into a very different sort of carcass. It shocked me, in the way a child is shocked by things that are not fair. But what is fair is something kings decide.

When he was done, Bodhbh raised his wand above his golden head and crooked his mouth.

'And now,' he said, 'we shall begin the punishment.'

Lir moistened his lips and his eyes raked across my face, hungrier for my blood than he had ever been for my poor body.

'Aífe, what is the worst thing that could happen to you?' asked my foster-father, smiling as gently as if he were running his fingers over the soft ears of his hound. And he pulled it from my throat as though it were a string of beads that I had swallowed. My voice was raw, and all my need laid bare.

'Never to … meet my family again … never to feel the earth … never to end … for me to be alone, alone with who I am and what I have done, for ever.'

'Oh,' he said to me, 'I think we can do a little better than that.'

And then he set to work.

This magic was as old and dark as the earth itself, but it was colder and sharper. There was no nuance. No sense of shaping or weaving. He wanted something to happen, and it happened in the bluntest and most direct way it could. Our people are not easy to kill, but what was done to me would have killed me, if he had not taken pains to ensure that it wouldn't. When I passed the threshold of tolerance, where I began to lose consciousness, I was nudged awake. He melted me into a sort of dough and set to work on me, to ease the lines of my back and neck at a crooked angle. To elongate the front of my face and deepen my eyes. When he was finished, and it felt like he never would be finished, almost no-one registered the wrongness of what he had done, the monstrosity, and I realised that it had all taken place in the blink of an eye. Time had stopped still, so that he could hurt me.

Lir's face was pale, aghast, though. He had seen that show of strength. That warning.

I tried to get up, but my legs, such as they were, would not touch the ground. They could not find purchase. I reached again and rose a little further into the air. I had to keep my muscles tense to stop myself from being pulled this way and that. So many little currents I could feel.

They pulled on me like strings. My body hurt.

'You will be a demon of the air, Aífe, for your crimes,' Bodhbh said in front of everyone. 'You shall never know the Otherworld, but will have no relief from who you are and all that you have done. You have brought shame on the name Oillill of Aran, and you and yours will be known as traitors and deceivers, quick to scheme against their betters. My company are already on the trail of your sister and will do her the mercy of a swift death.'

I gasped, and the sound of it was horrible.

'You have left the swans the gift of speech,' Bodhbh said. 'It is a gift I leave to you, as well, but I will not grant you the gift of being heard. No-one shall see you, no-one shall look at you. But when you are there, they will know that there is something close that is hateful and will leave you quickly. You will be friendless and alone. A warped and homeless thing, uneasy in your skin. You refused to accept your place in the world and now you shall have no place, in this one or the next.'

My lidless eyes flickered on his face. The stern line of his mouth crooked up a little. Oh, he was enjoying this. My anger began to boil in me again. If I could place my little claw upon the earth, perhaps. But I could not, and even trying hurt me.

'Now, LEAVE!' he said and with a flick of his hand he brought a cruel wind into the room, to lick at his cloak and tumble me out into the great wide skies.

And so I went.

SCÉAL

There was a camp set up by the shores of Loch Dairbhreach, so that Lir and Bodhbh the Red could pay visits to the Children of Lir. Indeed, so sweet was the music and company of these fair swans that many people came to converse with them and listen to their enchanting song, which could soothe a man to sleep, no matter how many worries he had inside him.

TINNE

how do you
learn to live
inside a skin

an element that isn't really yours

The leaves are shining in the pale cold light. When I could walk through the wilderness, through places where no paths had yet been worn, my feet on the ground and my skin shrinking on my bones with the chill of the wind, I felt alive. When Lir would touch me, in the way that husbands touch their wives, I felt alive as well. At first, I mean. I mattered. I was here. I was still here.

Away from other people, in the wild, I needed no-one's touch to give me that. And when I returned to stone walls and cold faces, I would have twigs and sticky little seeds, dried leaves, the husks of insects, little stones all gathered in the fabric of my cloak, the waves of my hair. Sometimes I would find the smallest wounds, little cuts I hadn't even noticed, pocking my skin. A thorn or two clinging underneath the surface that I would have to dig out with the slender pin at the back of a brooch.

I wish that I had gotten what I needed, that feeling of being present, or mattering, from the children of Aébh. They never ran to me the same way that they did to their father, the same way that they would have to their mother. When I was there with them, I felt like staff. They looked at Lir as though he were a god. But I was always closer to a mortal.

When we were little girls, no-one held us, so we held each other. I could hold someone to me. Could stroke their back or tickle my fingers down the soft curve of their arm.

I could tell them it would be all right.

That was a skill I had, back then at least.

But I wasn't good at getting from confusion to intimacy. How can you force that love out of yourself? Hearts are not teats. I was, at times, fond of the children. I worried for them sometimes. I recall Fionnuala having bad dreams, as a girl. Sharp dry dreams and she would wake up gasping for a gulp of cold fresh water. And I would stand close to her and look at her. As though she were a carving on a wall and not a child in pain, but something in me waited for permission to go to her in comfort. And that permission never really came.

I made, in ways, a stranger of myself.

And wondered, later, if I had been the thing inside her dreams. It could have been so. I did become a monster. Cruelty was never far away. And I wonder if there had been a core of something in me. That made the best of things. That moved away from wanting and just tried. Do people learn to love by being loved? I didn't have the instinct for it as Aébh did, or even Ailbhe. She fought for our people, fierce beside her comrades. I had taken that away. Removed her from her tribe. The life she'd built.

And though I was a wild, misshapen thing, I still felt that small hand reaching out. But to my sister now, and to Aébh's children. They anchored me. What I had done was real. I'd made an impact. And there was a strange egotism to that, a sort of lordliness. At least at first. In some ways, Bodhbh and I weren't unalike.

I gathered shards of people. Stories, pieces. To try and make some sense of who I had been and was. And as my people faded from the hills, as our stones were broken and our trees uprooted, I tried to gather everything in me. And I tried my best to understand the different kinds of love. To work out where I'd failed. What had gone wrong.

And I was not the only one who suffered in my story.

And my story was not the only one with suffering.

It soaked the clouds like rain.

The hills like blood.

SCÉAL

Three hundred years passed quickly and pleasantly for the Children of Lir, until one day Fionnuala realised it was time for them to move on, to the wild and deadly Straits of Moyle. So they bid a heartbroken farewell to their poor father, and to the lake that had become their home, stretched their great feathered wings and set out across the skies.

FEARN

I knew what I was doing and I did it

the least I could do
to bear witness
with my lidless eyes

Stories that we tell begin with people.

This is one where everyone gets hurt.

It is a love story.

Etain was the most beautiful woman in the world. But beauty is different things to different eyes, in different mouths. She had gold-bright hair, wild red hair, raven black hair, pale skin, dark skin, golden skin. Her eyes green brown violet grey hazel blue, but always shining. She was slender, she was curvy, she was lithe and tall as a willow, or a sort of tiny living doll. She was the shape the teller covets most. Eyes looked on her and wanted. A gift. A curse.

Midir was a chieftain. He looked upon Etain. They fell in love. Though love means different things to different people.

Everything.

Or nothing much at all.

Midir had a wife. Her name was Fuamnach. She doesn't come off very well in the story. A jealous creature. As though jealousy were something you could help. What would a decent wife have done instead? Let him go, and loved him. Disappeared. Only spoken well of him, and been faultlessly polite when encountering Etain. Been accused of coldness, been at fault.

Fuamnach, in her anger, wove a spell that turned Etain into a fly. I know the rage that took. The mark it left. And the feeling of wrongness that seeps in when it becomes apparent that, after everything you gave and all you did, it didn't work. There is no way to make a world that wasn't built for you be fair to you.

Etain, infuriatingly, became the most beautiful fly that had ever been seen, the size of a man's head, with eyes like jewels, her iridescent wings as beautiful and intricate as the finest lace. Her buzzing was a sweet and soothing melody. Midir remained enchanted.

Fuamnach resolved to try harder and summoned a spell to make Etain smaller and more helpless, a raging wind to drive her far away.

And when Midir saw what she had done, he was heartbroken, and Aengus Óg, whom you might remember, Bodhbh's brother, Caer's bird-lover, went to Fuamnach and cut off her head.

And then, there wasn't any more she could do. Sometimes heads speak in stories, but generally when they have wisdom to impart, murders to solve. When somebody will listen. Fuamnach's head was silent. Her body still. Her jealous heart was stopped. She had been punished.

Once Bodbh has done his worst, my part in the Tale of the Children of Lir that people tell is at an end. What happened next to me is of no consequence.

But I am hiding in between the lines.

I watched them. Of course I did, whenever I was able. Wracked with guilt and that same jealousy still too. That I couldn't help. To see their people looking at them, thinking of them, when I couldn't even close my eyes to sleep. When I couldn't rest my feet upon the earth.

There was nothing, no-one I could touch.

It took me more than a century to work out how to use my wings. I couldn't fall, so there's the absence of that pull to earth, and the wind is a mercurial thing. You think you can rely on it, and then it changes, moves you somewhere else.

Just like a heart.

When I learned to fly first, I tried to fly up, up beyond the air, to the dwelling place of the stars. I thought that I could end my life that way, perhaps. Could freeze, or choke, or break up into nothing, into pieces. But the heavens are not for the likes of me, and the air was a prison as well as a curse. It kept me tethered to it. It pulled me back. I could not stop myself.

On I went, cursed to drift, to be pushed and pulled about by the winds, as the children were cursed to stay in one place. And I found my way to them, when I could. It was a strange sensation. Like a person keening on a battlefield, or a warrior looking grimly on. Work had been done, and it could not be undone. But it was important to see it. See what happened. Because they were the children of my sister, and I had hurt them, and I was ashamed. There was a sort of mercy in not being seen, I thought then. I had a horror of their small, black eyes.

Loch Dairbhreach is very different now to what it was, but some things are still the same. The dusty fresh smell of wet things drying. The life that teems inside, the little flicker of fish and insects. Water-spiders busy at their work. I have learned, over time (and so much time), to get close enough to things to look at them and wonder at them. Our world is still so intricate.

Big blue creatures with iridescent wings still swarm at Loch Dairbhreach, beaded looking insects, dancing in the air between the wilderness and the water. Sometimes they mate with each other, two lines that form an oval in the air, twisting and flickering around, intent. It was not a bad place for me to give them, and they had some solace there for a time. They were children, and they stayed as children there. Watched over by grown people, watching beards turn grey and troughs develop under people's eyes.

Like Fuamnach, jealous of a fly, I found myself looking upon them with spite in my heart. Spite and guilt mixed. Those swans had comfort. And when they raised their heads and made sweet music from those long white throats, beaks opening like oysters and chests filling with sweet, soft air, all I could think on was the sleep that I would never have.

Paths emerged over the years through the long, thick grass and arrangements of stones, for fires and making food. Lir spent time there often, and his new wife was there by his side. Sometimes I looked at her face and saw Ailbhe's face. Her belly grew and the swans bent their heads to it and sang to it sometimes. I wondered how they felt about that, and if they spoke the one to the other when nightfall came and they retreated through the tall, thick rushes fat as fingers to their nest where they slept, much as Aébh and Ailbhe and I had done in the house of Bodhbh the Red. Fionnuala at the centre, Fiachra on one side, Conn on the other, and Aodh before her. I would look at them, from a distance. At the routine they had built for themselves, and the ache in my heart at all they had that I would never have was still there.

I could not escape the dark side of my nature. I longed for fairness, but for myself particularly. When I had been a noblewoman, I had not thought of the stomachs of the attendants around me, the people on the land and those who served us, of their lot in life. I had assumed that everyone was happy except me. And, while I was closer to the life before my life, I would often still find myself assuming that. I would look at stories of other people who had done worse, fared better. I would tell myself their tales and wish for peace. Peace, however, is a thing to want, a job of work.

In the dark, sometimes, when everyone had gone, though, one or other of the swans would rise, pale as a cloud, and glide across the water, waddle out to one side or the other of the lake, across the shore, where dead rush-husks, as pale and hollow as old bones, cracked beneath the weight of them. Their flat grey feet would slap undignified a little bit away from the lake, towards the woodlands. And I would follow them, and I would look. And they would raise their black eyes to the moon and stars, the drops of milk the sacred cow had scattered all across the heavens to guide and nourish us, and the sounds they made then would be lonely ones and sorrowful and not at all like music. And my heart would recognise something inside those sounds and I would ache at their sorrow and all that they would never know or have.

Feelings are complicated things, and hate and love were hand in hand so often in me then. Both have faded over time. I did not spend long with the swans, on Loch Dairbhreach, as any time I rested too long in any one place, it was as though the air itself would report back to Bodhbh, and I would feel a sudden slap that left me reeling, sent me somewhere else entirely, and it would take me time to force my way towards that lake again.

In the absence of companions, I clung to the sight of those creatures of water and of air I had created. I clung to the things I had done, because there was so little I could do, save to exist and suffer.

Suffering is not unique to me. The stories my people tell run thick with it. We are hungry, it seems, for other people's losses, rages, hurts.

My curse was being lonely, gathering snatches of story on the wind. Learning to lean closer, to look closer. Straining for the want of being seen.

What had been mine to touch was now denied me.

And I kept reaching for it nonetheless.

It was so close.

Water-lice move under the pebbles in the water. Beaks flicker in and out, bodies dive in and don't surface for ages. You have to hold your breath and count the beats.

Fionnuala often made a game of it, of who they had become. And Aodh pretended that it worked. Midir won his prize. And then he lost. You can't protect a heart. No matter what.

Nine hundred years. To wait for old gods to die and new ones to be born. For north and south to wed. I still wasn't sure what the words I had spoken to them on the lakeshore meant, but it was clear that a long time would pass before their curse was ended. It was too much to bear, for any creature. I watched them as the air stung my dry eyes, and the air grew thick around the lake. Time was slipping by and fear was building. They exist to be their father's sorrow. Even their pain is his. There is a trap in that. There is a trap in everything, if you look at it clearly enough.

I wonder sometimes what would freedom even look like for them, as opposed to what they got. Those first three hundred years, they dreamed of going back to normal life, I think. They certainly seemed chained to it, the goings and the comings of their father, the people around the lake who clamoured to them, for them. Celebrity, you'd call it now perhaps. There were parts of it they did enjoy. Fionnuala's white head and golden beak, tilted towards a handsome warrior, laughing and speaking. Forgetting the body she was living in, watching him steal kisses from a girl who was the same shape he was, more or less. Aodh watching the dancing, and waddling out of the water for an instant to join in, and then remembering that his grace on earth had ended. It was only on the water, in the air he could move beautifully. Chains grow heavier when they have been forgotten for a moment. Fiachra, neck swishing this way and that way as he watched a game of hurling. And Conn, who took to being a swan more quickly than the others, would often show them how to do things with their wings or beak. Which grasses to eat, which to avoid. Sometimes Conn would seek out other swans and spend time with them. I'm not sure if it was contentment or pragmatism, but it was different from the others in a way that surprised me. I had always considered Conn and Fiachra to be a unit, and their differences surprised me more than they should have. Perhaps I had not looked at them as closely as I should have, particularly with the twins. The grief I felt at Aébh's passing might have kept me from warming to them, or perhaps it was my grief, my inability to cope with the duties of motherhood when I still felt all the needing and wanting of a child. My inability to interact with them, or anyone, forced me to look at them outside of their relationship to me or Lir or Bodhbh, and consider who they were, all by themselves.

Watching them come into their own was interesting, but not without pain for me. The hum of the life they could have had always in the background of things, like a harper in another room, sometimes closer, sometimes far away. I would hear it sometimes, even when I was away from them, and it pulled me back again. To witness.

I had long known that freedom looked like death to me, but they did not know enough of life to crave that yet. I had ensured they would. And each time I returned to look on them, I felt a little of who they had been before had chipped away. The wilderness was building in their hearts. They still took comfort in the people that surrounded them, but more and more they clung together. Necks wrapped around necks. Breath mingling. There was more than one of what they were, though it was becoming increasingly difficult to perform a humanity they didn't feel. The little joys of their life on Loch Dairbhreach became something like taunts towards the end. Perhaps because they knew that what was coming would be harder. They would leave and only have each other. Nobody to mind them or admire them. I was there, but they didn't know that. And that was for the best. I had hurt them and was unable to help them. A useless creature, torturing herself.

Midir and Etain, as the story goes, had happiness, in stretches and in snatches. But happiness is finite. And my poor swans had to leave the lake where their father stroked and petted them. Where soldiers wept at the sweetness of their music. Where their tragedy was sculpted into something meaningful, instead of what it was.

A waste of time.

Their last night on the lake, the humming in the trees was loud and sweet. Lir's people spread honey on their beaks and their father stroked their feathers and told them that he loved them. He had been coming less and less to the lake. Every day turning into once a week, turning into once a month. They had other visitors and he was a chieftain. Our people were beginning to retreat inside the world at that stage and he was making plans along those lines himself. The woman he married after me died and he took another wife. More children now. And he would take them to the lake to swim and they would grab at the swans' big wings and laugh at them as though they were just birds.

And Fionnuala and Aodh and Fiachra and Conn remained gentle and understanding in a way that I would not have. I would have taken my big wings and hurt them. Would have snapped at skin with a sharp beak. I wasn't a very noble sort of person. The kindnesses I showed took effort always. And I do wonder about that, what it would have been like if Aébh's soft heart and my hard one had been evenly divided between the three of us.

There was no word of Ailbhe, and I took that to be a good thing. I kept my ears open and my eyes peeled. I found that washing them with rain helped and that there was another sort of relief that came inside me when the water beat down. It had come from the earth, you see, that water. Like us, in this world and the Otherworld and back again, it moved in cycles. And it was a mother's touch to me. And one I sorely needed.

I was still connected, in some strange way, to the world around me. And, when the screams that no-one heard rent the clouds and cut my throat to ribbons, when my reason left me for longer and longer periods of time until I found myself somewhere I did not remember going to, this was a comfort and a promise.

The berries on the holly trees bright as the fires that burned around the lake as the children of Aébh took flight. Sad songs inside their throats drawing tears from eyes like pus from wounds. And on the air, it faded, faded, faded. Until their soft white shapes had vanished. And there was only the moon itself.

I cracked the tight bones in my neck as I hovered close above the woods. I would catch up eventually. I knew where they were going. I had sent them there.

I watched the attendants stay and tidy up. Ashes and stones and footprints in the muck. White feathers in the reeds. But the lake belonged for ever to the children of Aébh, in that way that places woven through with story always carry the story with them. In the same way that I did. And still do.

None of us is just our own, but when you hurt someone, it marks you too. It becomes a part of who you are, the hurt you caused, and try as you might, it will always be there. And it will always be the truth. Sharp as a thorn and lodged inside you, underneath the skin.

Please protect them.

Aífe.

Oh, sister, I could not protect myself.

SCÉAL

The Straits of Moyle, between Éirinn and Alban, were fierce and cold on the children of Lir, and raged with many storms. The swans found themselves fastened to the rocks with the frost, or swept from each other with the fierce, wild winds. When storms died down, they would find each other at the rock of seals, Carraig na Rón, where Fionnuala would gather her brothers to her, Fiachra on her right, Conn on her left, and Aodh before her. They would lament the hardship and the pain and bemoan what had been done to them by their father's wife, their mother's sister. Over time, they learned to spend the day on the shore, where it was safer. But always they had to return to the cruel sea at night, and count the days and years until they could spread their wings and venture to the next place.

LUIS

you take salt inside your wounds

at the cost of some
thing gentle in you

Today it is a stretch to reach my story. I grasp at fragments, and I wonder if this is it. If I will become a senseless thing, and when that comes, if it will feel like freedom or loss. I think of the muscles in their strong wings working as they moved towards the Straits of Moyle and I think of blood and skin stuck to rocks. I think of the sharp bite of air and the warmth of soft white feathers against my leathered hide.

Chips and snatches.

Fat clouds that promise rain and that long, sweet wait for something like relief.

I am tired.

Aébh and Ailbhe.

I am tired, sisters.

Everyone I knew when I had fingers has turned in to dust and the rocks that marked them have almost all been flattened.

I feel something approaching. Like the horizon line where sky meets land. You can swoop and push but you can never touch a thing like that. It's always just a day or so away.

And is it my brain failing or trying to protect itself from the pain I caused in my own pain? Moyle will be hard to look at. But

I was there, and I have gone back since. And swallowed tears as waves lashed hard on rock. Bones broke and mended on the straits of Moyle.

And the children of Aébh were tested. Sorely tested.

And I did that to them, in my emptiness and in my rage.

A person's destiny is a funny thing, and even when they know the shape of it, it cannot be avoided, not for ever. I would think of Fionnuala's warm little body gasping in the bed and her breath misting in the air and me not going to her. Hovering like a raven at a carcass. Wanting to be sure that it was safe.

And never being sure.

Or feeling safe.

The soft brown earth teemed with life beneath the waters of Loch Dairbhreach, the lake of the oak. The oak is a powerful tree, for shelter and guidance. There was no shelter on the Straits of Moyle. There was no guidance. No people clamouring to touch their feathers or to hear their song. It could be a beautiful place. But it was the kind of beauty Lí Bán had when she pulled young men beneath the waves of Loch nEathach. They made a saint of her eventually. They liked doing that sort of thing, at one point. Claiming parts of us as parts of them. Building their new gods who spent infinity worrying about what people did with the little snatch of time they were afforded, instead of going about their own business, as if the world were only about the people in it and not its own strange beast.

I felt old then, and looked back at the jaded child that I had been when Bodhbh used his blackthorn staff to punish me with a strange mixture of loathing and amusement, as I look back now on the self I was then. The loneliness of it did drive me mad at times, and there were periods of time that I could not account for, when it seemed that I was just a body in the world, driven by instincts that could not be satisfied. There was no place to sleep, no bite that I could eat. There was only the air I breathed and those that could remember me.

And now there's only the air and my own self and I long for a time when someone knew me, to hate me or to spite me, even. I am trying now to remember who I was and who I am, and I claw at it as desperately as a cat scrabbling up a tree, away from the jaws of a hound, but when I get up there I do not like that either very much. No pleasing me.

The children, though at three hundred plus years they were grown now, persevered. And perhaps I had stranded them in childhood, like those men who used to go around trapping things in jars so they could kill them and preserve the corpses to learn from. I shouldn't judge too harshly. I too went back to the creatures I had hurt, time and again, hoping to glean some insight, or an answer to a question I couldn't quite put in to words, exactly.

The Straits of Moyle were as fierce and deadly as a hungry goddess. The water froze around the swans and they were fixed in place, a little bit away from each other and at the mercy of the wind, as strong as the beat of their own big wings that carried them from one part of their sentence to another. The swans would often find parts of themselves stuck to the icy slime on rocks they'd used for shelter.

And the wilderness of the seas brought forth a wilderness in the swans themselves. I observed them snap and peck at each other, sometimes ripping feathers from skin. They stopped speaking to each other in human speech and instead used a series of clicks, hisses, looks and movements to indicate their meaning. They would still sing, though. Every night they'd sing. It kept them bound together in the dark. If one drifted away, they would strain for them. There were no other swans there, and Conn felt the lack of them, I think. It was dangerous to be apart from each other, and so their strange closeness increased, a mixture of anger, sorrow, love and need. They shared so much, but they were different people, and had they grown up inside their father's home, they would have grown to want different things and to receive different sorts of futures the one from the other.

Fionnuala would have married well and run a fort with the precision and intensity she brought to protecting her brothers, I think. Aodh would have been a soft sort of man, in his head a lot; perhaps Lir could have shaped that into something respectable, like a healer. Fiachra would have been the most like his father. He always loved looking at other boys, at joining them. He would have wanted to be the big man, and I think he might have made a decent warrior, not a champion, but the sort who dies a death in battle that merits a single line in a ballad about someone with more skill and taste for slaughter. And Conn? Conn would have wanted to leave and build a home, I think. To have a family that was different to Lir's. To have children to love and a warm, good place for his people to sleep.

I tell myself the stories of their other lives, the lives that I would have had them live instead of what they got. And when I do, I try my best to make them happy ones, and I don't know why I do that, if it's to torture myself a little more, or to give them something in fiction that I could not give in life. A mother's love. A mother's fondness and hope. The things they needed I did not have in me.

On the stormy seas, there was always a possibility of losing each other. They had lost enough, and Fionnuala in particular hated the idea of her brothers being away from her, doing things she didn't know about and getting themselves into all sorts of dangers and torments. They planned that the rock of the seals, Carraig na Rón, would be their base where they would meet again, when the sea pelted and battered them the one from the other.

I wondered if they ever remembered Lir's men returning from the hunt with armfuls of bird wings, cut at the joint, to repair the magnificent thatch.

And there were softer periods, where their wounds healed and their feathers grew back. But they were always waiting for more pain. And I had done that to them. So I watched. Not for the full three hundred years, mind you. I left and I returned. I was trying to explain what had been done to me to myself. To work out the rules of it and the restrictions. I had noticed a weakening of the bonds on me, as though there were a chain around my neck that had once been pulled tight but was now only being held. I was interested in that.

Every time I tried to touch the earth, the constraints on what I was would hurt me, and I would take a long time to recover. I fashioned for myself a way to sleep. If I tilted my head back and filled my eyes full of rainwater, I could block my vision out a little with the sting of it and will myself to something like unconsciousness. It wasn't sleep exactly, and it did not revive me. But it felt like one in the eye for Bodhbh, and I was still a petty sort of thing.

When I blacked out, I would always wake somewhere unexpected. The air didn't hold me in place, and why would it. It could sense I didn't want to be there. That I had given myself to other elements, and like all unwanted things, it disliked co-operating with disrespectful creatures. I began, at that time, to notice other lives inside the air. The birds, the insects. Little darting things and strong, soft beasts. Sometimes I would try to join in a formation, to see if I could, but the revulsion that living things felt for me was strong and they would disperse and move away.

Aodh, Fiachra, Conn and Fionnuala could nearly sense me there sometimes as well. They would sometimes call out to the wind and give it my name and bring such curses down upon me that I would know them for their father's children. I did not wish to increase their discomfort, and kept my distance, in case they would sense that I was there and feel the disgust, hatred and fear that I inspired in any creature that I ventured close to. But then there was the night of the big storm.

The night when their song froze in their throats and salty ice worked its way through their feathers and through the tender meat of their skin to burn and wound them. The night when they were scalded by the cold as though it were boiling water. The night where the wind tore them apart, like the ribcage of a roast goose, pulling Fiachra, Conn and Aodh from Fionnuala, until all that was left was their last sad notes and the smell of their blood. If I had not sentenced them to live, that night would surely have killed them. There was no shelter, no respite. But a strange thing happened. I went to search for them, to see what had happened. And I felt none of that awkwardness that I had felt when they had needed me as children. Instinct took over, in a way it never had before.

I found Aodh, my little Aodh. And I wrapped my two big wings around him and pulled him up with me into the air. And though he could not feel me, he was sheltered from the wind and the rain. I am a demon. I am a strong creature. And I tried to listen for the mournful call of Fiachra and Conn. Fionnuala was still at Carraig na Rón. I knew that if she even had one brother, it would help her. She was the type who put aside her worries when she had others to worry for. No wonder then we didn't understand each other.

Aébh was like that, though.

Her graceful heart.

I didn't need my wings to float, as I could not touch the water or the earth. I don't know why he gave me them, save to let me know that I belonged to the air. So I guided my body towards the nearest swan, while keeping a tight hold on poor aul' Aodh. I used the sense of strangeness and fear to guide Fiachra and, when I found him, Conn back towards their sister. It took some time. We had to stop a lot, to keep them safe. As close to safe as possible. And it was a pity to me, the state that they were in when I found them. Conn's head hung and one wing was battered to no shape at all, Fiachra's breath was like a badly played fiddle, sharp and cruel inside his throat, and though it was hard to read their black-ink eyes, it was not difficult to interpret the screams and cries their sister made, of anguish and relief, as she drew each of them to her. And I was to release Aodh. I meant to. But the warmth of him had settled and I realised that he had fallen asleep inside the soft prison of my wings.

And so I held him close, as I had when he was small, and I murmured things about his mother, as Dechtaire and Smól had done for me, each in their turn. And he heard none of it, but he was beside me and content. And when he returned to his sister and his brothers, feathers smooth and shining, all unscathed, they greeted him like a miracle.

And it had been a sort of miracle for me. That there was still some kindness left in a world that was unkind. And that, strangest of all, it had come from somewhere in myself. I had spent the centuries arguing and picking at who I was. Trying to compose a story that would leave me blameless, or at least make sense of what I had done. But there was a refuge there, in me as well. A kind of peace. And I had found it once in the storm, when my thoughts were still and I was only focused on the pulse of Aodh, the warmth and the breath.

I had been a shield and not a sword.

Had kept him safe.

EABHADH

how do you stomach time that will not claim you

the world is big, and

won't remember you

remember that they

full of hidden things

That storm was the worst I witnessed on the Straits of Moyle, but there may have been others when I was away, exploring the air, and trying my best to find my sister, Ailbhe, in Alban. I found it hard to look on Scathach's island. A mist arose whenever I ventured too close, like a guardian had gently placed a strong hand on my shoulder and urged me to turn back, or it would go the worse for me.

There were stories of what went on there, of course, and I reached for what snatches of them I could, before people felt the chill of me and moved. The woman Scathach seemed to be skillful and mysterious in equal parts. A distant creature, people went to her, and spent time there, and then rejoined the world. She never did, though she did have daughters who ventured out into it. I admired that steadiness.

I journeyed with the air to other places too, where there were different sorts of people. I saw the Invaders, and what life looked like for them when they were not fighting us, and it looked much the same as our life did. And I looked at the bigness of the world, and all the magnificent things that were being built and done and remembered and forgotten, and the terrible thirst that had been on me was quenched a little. There was always more to know and learn. And it fed the want in me, bite by bite.

I returned to the Straits of Moyle a little over halfway through their time there. My nephews and niece had grown bigger and stronger than mortal swans and they had the mean look of feral cats who've had to fight their corner. A wary sort of belligerence. I had inhaled a breath of air from Sídh Finnachadh and held it in, and I exhaled it over them as a sort of comfort. My nephews turned to it and made soft sounds of pleasure. Fionnuala hissed, and opened up her beak, and spoke to them.

'What use is remembering what we had when we will never again have it?'

'Tell us about how it was before,' Fiachra asked of her, but Aodh nudged him with his long, soft neck, and he grew silent.

'We're not children any more,' Fionnuala said eventually. 'But we aren't adults either. We are birds and not birds. The sense she left us. It is a burden, surely ...'

'Sister ...' Aodh began, but trailed off.

'Fiachra, Conn, come close. And hear my story. There is a world in which we are just swans. Where we do not have to remember what we left behind. There was good to it, the taste of honey. But there were sharp things too. Our mother's death. We were too young, perhaps, to remember it, but all of us could feel it. Feel the lack of her inside our lives. When our father gripped us so close that his fingers bruised our skin, when we couldn't sleep at night for the sound of his hot breath, I often wondered would it be like this if she were here. Would I feel safer then inside myself?

'In the world where we were only swans, we were born from eggs. A clutch of eggs beside the glimmering lake of Loch Dairbhreach, with the oak trees and the apple trees. And we were small grey-brown things at first, that needed love and feeding, but we grew. We learned to swim through water quickly and carefully if needs be, and to glide for the pleasure of it sometimes as well. We learned to use our wings and beaks to ward off threats that came, such as they were. Otters and foxes and eagles and hounds.'

'And humans.'

'*Especially* humans. But our parents taught us well, and soon our feathers became white and our beaks turned gold, and we were three fine cobs and one fine pen. And we learned what plants were good to eat and ate them. The family would forage together, making sure that everyone ate well, and we would fly away to warmer places when it got cold, but return to where we came from when it was warm again. And maybe some of us would move from home, build new nests and have families of our own and teach them what we'd learned and keep them as safe as we could keep them. And in time, something would happen, and we would die, and be no more on the lake or in the sky or in the world.'

'And would the lake be still?'

'The lake would be as still sometimes as glass, and of an evening you could see the colours of the sky reflected in it, and hear the hum of all the lives around us. There would be insects and other birds as well, and fish below. And there would be creatures to be wary of. But not inside our family. We would be safe when we were by ourselves.'

And it was not raining then, but my eyes filled up with liquid anyway and drops of it spilled down into the Straits of Moyle and pooled, like an oil slick only I could see, on the surface of it.

'When will we die, Fionnuala?' asked Conn.

'Not for a long time, Conn. But until then we will mind each other like the parent swans mind the little cygnets and keep each other safe. And when I am sad and angry in my heart, like I am today and often, you will snuggle on my left and Fiachra on my right and Aodh before me, and I will feel like there is a place inside this world where I belong. Where I fit rightly. That is the gift my brothers give to me.'

And Fionnuala was talking to her brothers, but her eyes drifted to the dark patch on the water, and she pushed them from her and went over to it and poked it with her beak, and they moved away again from Carraig na Rón towards the shores of Ireland. And they stopped and let themselves rest at the mouth of the Bann river.

And it was convenient that they did, for soon the shouts of men broke the air. The four swans startled, raised their wings and necks for a fight. I noticed the patches of bare, scarred skin where feathers had not grown back at all and wondered what, apart from the elements themselves, had hurt them as badly as all that. The men dismounted, and put down their weapons, and approached, holding their hands out in a conciliatory manner. As though the swans were hounds that they could tame.

'Greetings, nephews and niece.'

There was a pause, and so he elaborated on his greeting.

'I am Aodh Athfhiosach, and this is my brother Fergus Fitchiollach. We are the sons of your grandfather, Bodhbh the Red.'

As graceful as her mother, as a queen, Fionnuala inclined her head very slightly and the boys relaxed around her. I eyed Bodhbh's sons, who had been born after my time. Two big strong men, and useless. A joker and a gambler. I had seen the like of them at court before. What had drawn them to the swans? I wondered.

A tale to tell, perhaps, while quaffing mead and making much of themselves.

I clicked my bones and stretched my own wings out wide, gliding on the air. The air responded when I asked for something more and more, and it was sometimes cool and welcome on the patchwork quilt of what I was, the rough scales and the feathers and the hide.

'You are welcome, uncles,' said Fionnuala, and her tone was arch, not that they'd grasp it, and the two big mouths of them open wide at the sight of an enchanted swan.

Magic was ebbing, even then, and their story had been told and retold, spoken of and sung of for centuries, even as it unfolded. Their cloaks were red and gold and their horses were white with golden bridles. Their hands were soft and their skin was smooth.

Luxury had sated them, and pleasure.

They had the look of babies after milk.

They exchanged pleasantries and told the swans that they were looking well. Which they were not, compared to what they had been. Conn asked about their father, and I tensed at the hope in his voice, not knowing what he hoped for. What is the right answer here? To have him happy or to have him sad? Neither is ideal.

Unsurprisingly, the boys did not stop to consider their answer. They spoke as though the swans were still children, and not five-hundred-year-old creatures who had not seen their family in centuries, though it was far from a hundred years it took to reach the shore, or send a messenger if they could not spare the time it took to think on them, in this harsh, dangerous place.

'They are well and happy, in the same fort together. Lir has a new wife now, again.'

I hissed at that, and my hiss met Fionnuala's as though they were wound around each other.

'And do they feast?' she asked, her voice as sweet as it had been the day I took her form and future from her.

'Oh, they do,' said Fergus, as though to reassure her. 'And listen to fine music and poetry, and dance and laugh. Your father is the soul of merriment, in spite of his great tragedy.'

'*His* tragedy,' said Fionnuala, and something dawned on the wide eyes of the sharper one.

'And yours as well, of course,' Aodh Athfhiosach 'the quick-witted' said to placate her, and the voice on him as oily as my tears had been.

Was his name given in hope, I wondered, for it did not seem to suit him very well. And Fionnuala snorted as though she had heard me muttering to her, and I startled at the strangeness of that.

'They do worry for you, for they have not heard tell of you or seen sight of you since the day you left Loch Dairbhreach. And it will be a wonderful consolation to them that we have found you here.'

'And have they looked?' Fionnuala's stance was defensive now and fierce. 'How long did it take yourselves to get here?'

'Little more than a day,' offered Fergus helpfully. Aodh nudged him. They both took a few steps back.

'Little more than a day.' Fionnuala's tone a smile before a stab. 'And how long, *uncles*, by your count, have we been here?'

She used the word 'uncle' as though it were the lowest, dullest thing.

Aodh shrugged. 'A long time. I am named for one of you.'

Aodh the swan looked at Aodh the man, and would have spoken more kindly to him, I think, had Fionnuala not continued.

'We have been here your entire life, and another life again, and another one besides that. Two hundred years or more. And we are tired. And we have no feather beds to sleep on, no soft roof to shelter us from storms. You bear the name of someone in the story we've become. Where were you when we thought Aodh was lost? When Conn's poor wing was twisted and torn? When we were still children enough to long for the comfort of our people?'

She spread her wings.

'Our curse might make a pretty poem to draw a tear or two at the end of a feast but it is written on our bodies. Who we are is suffering. Is this. And is there any sort of father who would leave his children hurting and drink his mead and sing and make more children? Your father is a king, the son of a god. And surely he could calm a storm or two. Build a shelter for us from the waves. Ask Manannán for help to keep us safe. There are things that they could have done if they loved us. But their love was only when to love us was easy. When we drew men to us and made sweet music. When they could garner sympathy from women. When we were close enough to touch. And when we moved from them, they turned their backs on us. And I see them, who they are. And I see you. Now LEAVE. Or we will give you scars to match our scars. Will see your blood mingle with our own inside the water.'

Fergus drew his sword.

'If we were things that could be killed by men, we would be dead already, child.'

'I am sorry,' said Aodh son of Bodhbh. 'I am sorry for your suffering.'

'You will be sorry for the time it takes to ride back to your father's *sídh*, if that. To pour a cup of wine. To fill your gut, and to share the parts of this story that suit you. The parts of us that you can bear to look at.'

The swans were all in formation now, hissing and clicking their beaks like snakes about to strike. It was a thing to behold.

And the riders slowly backed away, and mounted their horses with the golden bridles and the fierce eyes, and kicked their legs and beat a quick retreat.

And she looked up at the sky before she waddled back in to the water. At the place exactly where I was, and for a long time. And I could not read anything in her two black eyes, but I tried to send her some of my fury, to stoke her own.

To warm her in the night.

SCÉAL

When their time on the Straits of Moyle was at an end, the Children of Lir were glad to leave it. They spent the next three hundred years between Acaill and Iorrus Domnann and Inis Gluaire, and it was as cold and as miserable an existence as what had come before, until one terrible night, when the sea froze solid as stone between the two islands, and the swans were all caught in it, fastened to the waves like patches on a quilt. The fear stung through the Children of Lir like the bite of an eel, and though they could know no death while the curse was upon them, they feared what would remain of them as morning approached. And so they prayed to the new god, and in his mercy the storms eased, and morning broke. And their time on Iorrus Domnann was easier in the wake of that dreadful night.

RUIS

I don't know what I would have sacrificed for others

I have   taken more

than I   will ever give

and I am   still here

wishing I   could give

and only   taking

Of course, when those two hapless articles went home to their daddy, they were told that there was nothing they could do. That it would only hurt the swans to be seeing them and being reminded of all that they had lost. That it was a great sacrifice on Lir to stay away and very hard on him. But if he lived in the past, longing for the children he had lost, he wouldn't be able to be here for the people that needed him. And it all sounded very rational, and it reassured them that they were good people, who came from good people. That the right thing was being done.

And I felt a cruel tug on what passed for a spine in my demon's body that night. As though someone had been reminded of the inconvenience I had caused. It pulled me away, away, up towards the lands of snow and ice, where the air cuts like sheets of sharpened glass and the sky dances in colours the likes of which I'd never seen before. The joy I took in it surprised me. And I spent some time exploring, looking at the way the land met the water in delicate fingers, and how the trees grew differently. I waited until the hold on me relaxed a little and then began to journey back towards the Four.

It took time and effort, more than it should have. I had learned to let the air guide me and not to fight against it. I had time. And so did they, three hundred years, and more again besides. There were things they went through without me, but that has always been the case, from the very beginning. It would be disingenuous of me to pretend to be some warm, maternal figure. Guilt and familiarity were the two main pulls that drew me back, as well as that curiosity, that desire to know the story that has always been a part of who I am, for good or ill. On the way to them, there was one thing I witnessed that made me feel like all that we had lived was reaching its conclusion. That the old world was coming to a more final end, and that there would be a new thing now. And different.

I had never expected, through all those years of anger and hurt and longing, to see the death of Lir of Sídh Finnachadh. I wondered sometimes why I had gone for the children and not for him. I wasn't thinking clearly, and perhaps he seemed too powerful, too much. An adult, when I still felt like a child. Untouchable. I never let my brain make the leap. And I should have done. It would have made more sense than hurting innocents. Though perhaps it would not have even worked, if I had tried. Lir seemed fated to die in battle, which he did. A broad blue spear cast by Caoilte, son of Ronán. It drove what was left of his heart outside his body, and left a husk behind upon the grassy hills that people had called his but had only ever belonged to themselves.

I watched from a distance, inside as well as outside. It was as though I were watching someone recite a poem about what happened. I was finding it harder and harder to remember the great swathes of sensation I had had for Lir, and even the guilt for what I had done was becoming more distant from me. In time, that is what drew me back to the children of Aébh. That fear that what I had done to them would fall from me, like oak leaves to the ground as the air grew cold.

Lir left a hundred and fifty children behind to mourn him, including the four swans. And two widows. Myself and the girleen that he left behind. A wife seven hundred years younger than Fionnuala. We are almost at an end now, in the versions of the story people tell. The swans, of course, with three hundred years ahead of them, did not quite see it that way. I thought of them as I stayed for three days and three nights, watching warriors sack the *sídh,* until it was just stone on a grassy hill. Piles of feathers, pieces of treasures. The memory of screams. When a place's warriors are dead, all that remains are people with nobody to protect them.

It was a long and dreadful thing to see.

I did what small things I could do. Used the sense of dread to push a threat from them, or encourage them to move from something imminent. But in the throes of terror, more terror is hard to notice. People react differently. They freeze in place like deer about to flee, but never flee and only stare until it is too long. Sometimes they simply comply, accept whatever will be done to them and hope it will be swifter or softer because of that compliance. Some stand their ground and fight, and there are several futures that branch from that, many of them short. And some flee, take what's left of them and run and hide and hope they are not found. I don't think any one of those things works better than the other. When a person is in danger, it is the danger that is the danger and not themselves. And danger is unpredictable. It does not follow a set of rules or guidelines. I thought of the Four and of my own life there as I watched Sídh Finnachadh being pulled apart. It had been a beautiful structure, but so were the bodies of the children of Aébh and so was my body. Everything is brutal in the end. Even age.

My people did age, but it was much more slowly. Hundreds of years were to us as decades are to humans. We began to die when the new god wrapped his fingers round the land and squeezed. I have seen so many things end, and in longing for an ending to myself. Which I still find myself sometimes doing, not with the wide void of hopelessness I had when I was younger, but with clearer eyes.

The longer you live, the more quickly time passes. But even the fleetest of years is a year. And suffering prolongs things. The islands off the west coast of Ireland were beautiful, but the waters were savage. The children of Aébh rested on the shores and rambled around the islands, eating grasses, building complicated nests that took time and planning. Conn had learned to weave and braid rushes quite expertly with his beak and the support of a wing. Fiachra helped him to keep things steady, the two white necks twisting and flowing beside each other.

Their time was coming to an end eventually, and they could see the shape of that end now, and looked forward to going where they would. Together or alone. Fionnuala must have hated the thought of the boys separating from her, for all that she liked her own space. Her protective instinct had hardened into something very particular over the years and she did not feel safe when she did not know where they were. The thought of them flying their separate ways must have been daunting, and it tended to come up when they were arguing about other things. Where best to take shelter. Who their father was. She had grown very negative about him, since their time on the Straits of Moyle.

She felt the sting of his abandonment. And she was worried that it would happen again, again, in turn with one brother after another until she was all by herself, alone. I could hear it in the snap of her tone and the quietness of her for days afterwards, of the time she took by herself to think. Though perhaps she was simply thinking on someone else, and I had begun to filter the way I was, the lonely parts of myself, into this strange creature I had hurt. She was much larger than a normal swan. They had kept growing, little by little, year by year, until they were not as large as humans, but as tall, including their necks. They varied in size a little, as humans tend to do also. Fiachra and Fionnuala were the biggest, and Aodh the smallest. I wondered if that would have happened anyway, as they grew, or if something in the spell, something in my sense of who they were, had made that happen.

It must be that way with parents and their children. Looking at the parts of them, and wondering what is because of you, and what is their own. I have watched so many babies grow and change, in hospitals and fields and parks and gardens across the world. Sometimes I will stay fixed in one place for years to watch the changing face and body of a certain person. To see where they end up. How they die. I have seen so much death over the centuries. And still I am no closer to my own.

I try my best to protect people sometimes. When I can. It was while the Four were in the last three hundred years of their sentence that I began to come in to my power again. I had grown to respect the air, and work with it, and listen to what it wanted. And I remember listening closely to the wind in the leaves of the beech trees on a field near Sídh Femuin, where I grew up. And the more closely I listened, the smaller I felt, the edges of my body pressing in to each other, until I was the size of a cat, a crow, a blackbird. And I looked at my wings and spread them wide and they were small.

And I remember thinking.

Huh.

What sort of thing is this?

I placed a tentative claw upon the branch.

And landed.

And what a gift it was, to feel my feet on something. And I stayed there, grateful to the air and listening to all the goings on, the sap, the sunlight filtering into the leaves, the movement of water and air, the dance of the insects up and down and in and out across the bark and around the leaves. And I was smaller than I had ever been and it was a warm day and I could feel the sunlight on my feathers and it settled me. Underneath the tree was the earth and inside the tree was the water and the air was blanketing around me and it had done me kindness. What a kindness to be in the world and see the little pieces of it.

The sun set and rose again, and I stayed on my branch, afraid to leave it in case the feeling would end, and sometimes even with good, sweet things I start to see them with different eyes, and they twist into darkness and mistrust. I look at a mother holding her baby and I see the lines around her eyes and the twist of her fingers against the little ribcage as she bounces him on her lap and I think of those fingers squeezing. Squeezing the life away. And I think of how life is. And even the gentlest, kindest touches can't protect a person from that, can they? Sometimes there isn't space in me for breath and it's just empty, and this, this day, this night was only breath and wonder. Only life.

And when I felt the little press of air against my wings, I leapt back up inside it and my self rolled out to its enormous size, the splendid heft I have. And it didn't feel any more like the shape that had been given to me.

It was the shape I took.

The shape I was.

I had looked on the air as a cruel element, but it was full of other things as well, of life and light, and it had not asked to be my punishment. It was giving me back what it could give. Bodhbh the Red had died, as the sons of gods sometimes do, or forgotten me, the same way he had forgotten about the swans, once they failed to be of use to him. People will find other things to love. We have a bank of it to share with others, and when it gets too hard to keep on loving, sometimes we spend the coins we have in other places. My foster-father could be terribly cruel and terribly petty. But I had seen him be kind, too. Resolve disputes kindly and carefully, make sure that vulnerable people were taken care of.

And if I am more than the worst thing I have ever done, then so is he.

And so is Lir as well.

I am very old and my memories are failing, and maybe that is what death will be for me. Maybe one day, I will shrink into the size of a small bird, and forget I ever was a girl, and live and die and find myself not back inside this demon's body but somewhere else. And it will be like in the story Fionnuala told her brothers, where they were only swans and it was simple and good.

The changing and shifting of the air around me was similar, I think, to what happened with the children as well. I had been, for hundreds of years, wracked with an awareness of what I had done to them, and once I began to feel more connected to the world around me, and to have a sense of belonging, and potential, I wondered if there was anything left of what had been my power. I reached for it sometimes, and found wisps of this and that, but nothing I could get a hold on really. Nothing that would save me from the consequences of what I had done. I suffered on, as the four swans did among the islands, and I watched them and I didn't watch them. One year, I arrived to find six smooth white stones tucked into a nest beside the shore. And Conn, with his funny-shaped wing, was finding feathers and soft things to keep the nest snug, and sitting on it for longer and longer periods of time, until the night came and they had to return to the water.

And Fiachra hissing at him that *they died*, but as to who they were and what had happened, I never learned. There is no whole story. There is only what I experienced and what they experienced.

And those are often very different things.

I cannot know.

The night that they were supposed to have converted to Christianity in the story, there was a horrible storm. I was whipped around above the clouds and had to work very hard to stay near them. I tried to connect with the air, but it would not listen to me, being focused on the beating it was giving to the earth and sea. I tried to reach the four of them, but I could only watch.

And it was Fionnuala's voice, rising over the seas, that renounced the gods they had grown up with, who had abandoned them. Fionnuala had a great way for complaining and ordering people about, in the way that leaders often do. And she had her wings around her brothers, and they spoke words to the storm that whipped around them, and they asked it not to hurt them any more and it would have their loyalty and devotion. And the storm still whipped around.

'We need new gods,' said Conn, 'with different shapes. Who have kinder ways of doing things.'

'Aífe said that when her gods were dead we would be free then,' said Fiachra. 'Maybe we should pray to whoever comes next.'

'I don't want to pray to gods,' snapped Aodh. 'I can't see them, or touch them, and they have certainly abandoned us. Let us instead pray to the water that keeps us, the earth that welcomes us, the air that holds us and the fire that grows inside us with each new hardship.'

'That fire could burn the world.'

'I know it could.'

And so the swans, all together, prayed to the things that they could believe in. The elements and each other. Aodh and Conn prayed to Fionnuala, Fiachra prayed to Aodh, Fionnuala prayed to all of them around her, and their mother, Aébh, as well. They prayed in their haunting sing-song human voices, letting words and images swell and dip from their long white throats as surely as a strong bird flying across the landscape. And I let my voice join theirs as well, and begged any power that I had loved, or that had ever loved me, to be as gentle with them as they could and ease their torment.

And when I prayed, I had a memory of being a child again and on my back. On the soft grass, beside the girls I loved. We would draw pictures with our fingertips and make up different futures for each other.

I would be a druid, and Ailbhe a warrior. Aébh would be a queen, a wife, a mother.

We would see our family again.

And they would welcome us with open arms.

My love, they'd say to us, *my little love. How we missed you! Welcome, welcome home.*

None of us could have the future now that we had wanted. But that didn't tarnish the memory. If anything, it gilded it. I remembered that love and that connection, and I felt it again through them, in them. And it nourished me that night. And when the storm broke, and the sea was still, I think each of us knew, somehow, in as much as you can know a feeling, that the world around the four of them would be a little safer from here on out. And Conn began to look for the six stones, and Fiachra, Aodh and Fionnuala helped him until they found the same ones again, known by their smoothness and the markings on them, and they rolled them with their beaks towards the nest, as tenderly and surely as though they had been their own.

And when the nest was fixed, they looked upon it, and Conn getting ready to roost. And Aodh asked if anyone had heard the other voice when everyone was praying.

And Conn nodded, and Fiachra as well.

'Who do you think it was? Was it a sort of god?'

Fionnuala, giving nothing away, told them not to worry about that now and to keep going with finding things to eat and a sheltered place to sleep that hadn't been battered into pieces by the waves. But she looked up at the clouds for a long time that night and I wondered how much she had heard of what I'd said. And if she'd recognised the voice that spoke the words. I couldn't exactly tell myself if I still sounded like myself. I'd only heard my voice from the inside, and I hadn't spoken in so long. There had been no reason to. No other person.

Her voice rang up into the sky.

'Stay away from us.'

I heard it as surely as if her head had been resting in the curve of one of my wings, that close, that loud. It shocked me. Her power was growing.

And she knew enough of who I might have been to want me gone.

And so I left.

For years.

And years.

And time passed.

SCÉAL

Their time on the islands came to an end, and the Children of Lir were happy and excited to return home after their long confinement. 'Come,' said Fionnuala to her brothers, 'we will return to Sídh Finnachadh, and see Lir and his household, and everyone who loves us.'

And so the Children of Lir set out, upon the wing, and flew lightly and gracefully towards the Sídh of Finnachadh, where they had grown, until their childhood had been stolen from them. But when they got to their father's place, the hill was deserted and empty, the ruins of what had been covered in nettles and hawthorn trees and honeysuckle.

No fire on the hearth, no arms to embrace them.

And the swans keened their sorrow loudly through the night.

IFIN

a place is not what's built upon a place and home is not a carcass

picked apart and littering the grass

there is no honey there is only blood

there

is

you

no who you were

can't go back

I respected Fionnuala's wishes and left them to themselves for many years, going about my solitary business, and watching other people begin and grow and die, and wondering about everyone that I had left behind and if they were alive now, or only memory, returning just as their sentence was ending on the islands. My curse on them was coming to an end, and I had to know what happened once it did. Magic wrought in anger, I had not thought about the ending, really. I had been caught in a trap and would have done anything at all to get out. Of course, I knew by this stage that they had not been my gaolers, for all the sight of them could be frustrating, jarring me away from all this world I'd been seeing, towards the kind of person I had been when I was in it.

There are some people who in desperate circumstances will think of others, seek to give them aid. I was not one of them, in life, nor in this form I take, though I can reach out sometimes and effect small changes, be the dark feeling that stops someone walking down a dangerous road, the sense of dread that pulls a driver sweating towards the side of the road, the feeling that someone mistakes for guilt and changes course. But with big disasters, I can do little. Horrible things happen every day. I see them happen sometimes. Here I am. It can be frustrating, to want to help, to need to atone and to see no way to make that happen. It was sharper when I was younger, mind. There is a sort of distancing that happens. And when I look at people now, I do not see myself. I am another sort of thing entirely. I find it hard to be appalled by things that have happened over and over and over again. That will keep happening. Earth can be poisoned, dug up and destroyed. Wars are waged. But it is only a part of a thing and not the whole story. There are always little shards of love, or calm or kindness. I find them too, within the sharp, cold air. And at the time, nine hundred years after I had held the wand of bone above my head, my two feet on the wet ground and fire in my heart, I had something like hope. That there was a way this would unfold where the Four would find something like happiness. Or ease. A soft, safe life for a time, to make up for the lash of the wind.

I wondered, and I hoped. What I could never have, I hoped for them.

Would they return to what they'd been before? Minds as old as stones in children's bodies? Would they simply crumble into dust? I had to know, I had to know how guilty I should feel. How it would end, or would it end at all. If I could touch things, and locate that wand, perhaps there would be a way. But when the air let me be a bird and not a demon, my thoughts became the thoughts of a bird. I was guided by the shape I took, in the way the children might have been had I not left them with hungry hearts that longed to change their lot, that knew to hate it.

They had found a way to be the one beside the other for nine hundred years, and of course they had. They were the only ones of what they were and I had bound them there, much as I wish that I had not. Much as sometimes I wish that one or other of the attendants had taken the hint and taken the blade and slain me when I asked it of them. I was a noblewoman and the wife of Lir, either of which might have meant their death. But death is only the opening of a sort of portal, and then the whole thing starts again, again. I do not know. Perhaps I would have been born somewhere else and always been a lonely sort of person. Perhaps I would have lashed out in a different way if I had been a druid, a queen, a champion. Circumstances change, but I do not know that anyone can ever fully escape themselves. To be the kind of person that you don't need to escape from is the key, perhaps. But how much of who you are can be helped is still a mystery that eludes me.

When the Four realised that their time had come to an end, they hummed with expectation and nothing changed. But that they flew away. They had stopped trying to do so after Moyle, and perhaps they could have broken the curse sooner if they had. But what a person could have done is a knife, and I am glad they didn't let it cut them. They followed the rules that I had set for them. And up into the sky they went. Slowly, achingly slowly. Conn's twisted wing holding them back, they returned to the home that they had known when they had eyebrows, teeth.

Fionnuala had long nursed a desire to speak with Lir about his treatment of them and berate him in the way she enjoyed berating about things that did not please her. In some ways she was more his child than any of them.

As they bade goodbye to the islands I followed them, above the layer of clouds, far enough away for them not to sense my presence.

And when they saw what had become of their old home, they wept, not in the manner of swans but human tears, as angry and salty as the Straits of Moyle, and their bodies twisted the one around the other and warped as cruelly as a hawthorn tree, twisting and moving as though battered by a wind I could not see, that was not there.

'He never came to say goodbye to us,' said Aodh.

'He said goodbye to us for three hundred years at the shores of Loch Dairbhreach,' said Conn. 'Every time he saw us in our bodies, and heard our voices coming from these throats, his face said goodbye. He looked at us like memories.'

'Like corpses.'

Fionnuala looked at Conn for a long time.

'I see that.'

'It was easier for me to see. I never fit easily inside the skin that I was born with.' And Conn stretched out his wings and the one that had been twisted was a different shape to the other one, but they were both so white they were tinged with blue, and there was a glow around them. A glow around each of the Four, and I felt shaken with something between tenderness and awe.

They had survived, in spite of everything that I and the elements had thrown at them. And their difference had become a sort of strength.

And it had nothing to do with me, and everything to do with themselves, and the blood that coursed in their veins. The blood of Oillill of Aran, of Aébh the loving, and of Lir as well, whose bull-headedness may have served them well, over the centuries.

'Where will we go now that there's no home?' asked Fiachra, and his voice was very small and very low. I pictured him crying beside a broken twig he had been using as a sword, remembered finding the tree that it had come from in the forest, making him another, only to find that it had already been forgotten. I resented him for that, bitter at the time ill-spent on pleasing someone who could please himself.

The four swans curled on top of the hill, among the rushes and the purple heather, where the earth is damp enough for frogs and soft enough to squelch underfoot. And they sang a dirge for all that had been lost. Harsh and guttural at first, then potent as a spell, it reached around them, through the earth and sky. And the fire was in them too. They had survived this, and they mourned together. For all that had been lost and what they had found about the people they had loved.

That was a thousand years ago and more, and their story ended long ago, somewhere in the middle of mine. There is a carpark and a sort of metal tower on the site where Sídh Finnachad once stood, and people burn their waste and eat their chips there. But the heather and the rushes and the little golden frogs and swarms of ants still remain. Many things at once, like every place and every little life. I perch, if the air allows it, and I raise my voice to the heavens. I speak to people who are long since dead, to the Four, to Lir. I speak to Aébh and Bodhbh. I speak to Dechtaire and Smól. I speak to Ailbhe, whom I never found, with all my curiosity. There are losses that you can't avoid.

Four bright bodies, on the soft green and rough purple.

And the screams of them.

For all they had endured.

And for fear as well.

Of all that would come after.

SCÉAL

The Children of Lir slept on the hill where their childhood home had been, and it was a sorrowful sleep indeed, and more sorrowful again when they woke from it and were reminded of all that had been taken from them. The sun rose over them, and they looked out over seven different counties, then opened their wings and took to the skies, towards the Lake of the Birds on Inis Gluaire. There they stayed for a long, long time, and life continued as it had before, until Holy Patrick came to Ireland and began to spread the Christian faith.

ÚR

old hard   things like

prayers   stones

and   ghosts

there is no satisfaction seeking answers from

When the story of the children of Aébh is told, they polish it up and cover it with the lessons that they most want you to learn. Faith and hope and tragedy being the fault of one bad person. Things begin, and things end as they were supposed to end. And this didn't really. After the nine hundred years, there they were, not bound together any more by the curse, and so they separated, and each went their own way for a time. Fionnuala bound them only to this promise: that in ten years' time, they were to return to Inis Gluaire, where she would be waiting, and that they would spend some time together there again, before venturing on into the future.

At that time, they were uncertain as to what would happen. If they would be swans for ever, now, or if they would just have to die. And they were unsure what could kill them, also. For they had survived so many things that hadn't.

Fionnuala went to Sídh Femuin, to see what was left of their grandfather, Bodhbh the Red. And I followed her. Aodh went to warm waters, off the coast of France, and Conn into the wilderness round Ireland and Alban. With his wing the way it was, he couldn't rely on it to get him back. And vows mattered to the children of Aébh, as they did to our people. Names and vows were more important once. Or they should have been. There were always those who valued power more than their word.

Fiachra just began flying, as far and as fast as he could. His powerful wings fiercely beating through the air, making me realise how much he had held back when he flew beside his siblings. The confidence of him, like a warrior carving his way through a battlefield, or a player outstripping all around him for the ball.

I followed Fionnuala, because I knew they would return to her in time. And because I, too, wanted to see what had become of Bodhbh. There were no answers in that place, however. Her two webbed feet on the dry ground, growing dry themselves, outside of the water. Eventually, she began to speak. And she told the story of the Children of Lir. And it was somewhere between the one that Bodhbh began and the one that I have tried to put together. And it sang with deep anger, and deep love. She sang the life she would have wanted to live, if she could have lived a life on her own terms. And what she wanted was her own. I will not share it here, for I felt fixed to the spot, but also full of awkwardness, hearing the wants inside her heart and how much they had in common with my own. In another world we would have been the sort of family that people think of when they think of family. The kind that isn't broken like a fragment of a vase or carved with complicated scars like stones in sacred places.

When she had finished singing her dreams and sorrows into the earth, I knew that afterwards it would be a sacred place to me, for as long as I had sense enough to remember. A sharp kind of sacred. For to look inside another life as deeply as I did is a burden as well as an honour. I carry her and who she is in my heart now. And, of course, I carry her siblings too. But the shape and size and detail of Fionnuala is more tangible.

She was the sort of person who would have been remembered in story, I think, no matter what path her life took. In the stories that are told today, she is the leader, and she holds it all together. Which is the truth, but the toll that takes. To always be deciding things for people. To shape their fates, to mask uncertainty with certainty. To weather storm after storm, and guide them through, and then be left behind. I think that Aodh, Fiachra and Conn broke her heart a little when they left her. And of course, they needed to. They did. Nine hundred years is such a stretch of time, even for me. But she had done so much for them, and the instant that they had the chance to go, they left. They chose themselves, when time and time again she'd chosen them.

She left bright blood and tears upon the stones of the place where Bodhbh's fort had been. And I used my power, then, to guide her to the little shelter that my sisters and I had used, when life was only for playing and singing and fighting and dreaming of all the things we wanted and would never ever have.

She curled up there, and slept so still, she could have been a little marble stone. Knowing she was used to the heat of her brothers, I tried to shelter her with my two great wings, but she didn't fully settle until I rose away, higher up into the air, until she was almost entirely hidden from my sight. Then my sharp ears heard the little sigh and small, soft snores.

SCÉAL

And so one day a follower of Saint Patrick, a holy man named Mochaomhóg, appeared on the island. He built a chapel, and he rang a bell, and sang strange and beautiful prayers, the likes of which the Children of Lir had never heard before. And they sang their own glorious song, and the holy man came to meet them, and they spoke to each other, and the four swan-children put their trust in the cleric and stayed with him in his abode and listened to the tales of the new god. And things were peaceful then for a short time.

GORT

kindness never comes without conditions

there is no shame in

and in the cold

have to do to stay

doing what you

The holy people came, as people do. Patrick was not the first of the Christian faith to visit Ireland, or even the most charismatic. He was persistent, though. Mochaomhóg lived a quieter life than he did, certainly, and is remembered in a quieter way. Both of them had dealings with what remained of my people, the Tuatha Dé Danann. My people lived in story and memory, their lives long lost and misremembered on the tongues of others. Shades of what we had been, before we had moved to the world beyond the world. (Why do I still say we, when I am unlike them now and have been outside of everything for such a long time? Perhaps something to do with belonging, with the need still to belong, with that small hand that reached across the ocean to Oillill and Éabha, while we three sisters cowered in that little boat that took me into this, to where I am.)

And they were clever, these people. They knew what people needed from the old gods, so they left traces. Bridget, Mary, festivals and wells. In the way of tricksters, they claimed to give, and sought to take. And some of them knew it, and some of them fervently believed what they were bringing. There are those who want to matter and end up leaving scars. I was one, once.

Fionnuala lived a quiet life too, on the Lake of the Birds. She moved around, built nests in different places. She met another swan, quite unlike herself, and she laid eggs. But when they hatched, they were just full of blood and bits of down. I thought of Conn, and wondered if anything like that had happened before. She tore the nest they had been in apart and drove the swan she'd paired with from the island. She was alone then for a long time. Not quite as long as their sentences had been, but when you're needing people and don't have them, the days can stretch out wide as jaws, and hungry for your misery. They fed well on hers.

I tried to help and called on what I could. The air did not turn me in to anything. When I moved close, she'd flinch, anticipating hurt. Like one of Lir's hounds.

And it was in that state Mochaomhóg came upon her. And I could tell by the baldy head on him that he was one of the followers of the new god, and by the gleam of something in his eye that he'd been hunting something. He was one of those small, quiet men who assesses everything. There was a stillness about him, a confidence. He was fat on the greatness of his god and his entitlement to the land around him. Bossing around the men who built his dwelling place, and demanding dinner and minding from the women. And it was sparse, of course. Nothing showy. But a fine strong chapel and a little hut, and didn't he sleep in the chapel when the hut got too cold, and accept baskets of this and that dropped to him like offerings to this new god most people didn't really understand as of yet, but who was growing in power and had to be obeyed, it seemed.

I didn't like the cut of him one bit.

A swan is a proud creature, but Fionnuala was not a swan, exactly. She was of a world before this world, and at this time, she was closer to a thousand years of age than to the girl she'd been when I had pulled her screaming from her life and turned her to a strange, unnatural thing. Her wings were silver at the edges in a way that a swan's are not, and her beak was paler than it had been, closer to a pinkish-gold than orange. And Bodhbh had kept the story of the Children of Lir alive enough, during his reign and after, that it was still being recited around the fire then, while the four of them still waited for an ending, happy or otherwise. I think Mochaomhóg knew well who Fionnuala was. I think he had an angle. I can't prove it.

And even if I could, there would be no-one I could prove it to. I am alone.

And it is hard to be alone, and it was harder for Fionnuala than it has become for me, with time. Like the child I had been, she was used to having her siblings around her, but she had not lived long enough in the skin she was born in to have them taken from her, or to be taken from them herself. When Aébh was missing first, myself and Ailbhe found ourselves saving up things to tell her, saying, 'Aébh would love that' or 'Aébh will think this funny when she comes.' But firstly, she hardly visited, and then she was dead, but things that she enjoyed still happened all around us, and we would see them still, with our own eyes, surely, but also with the glassy eyes of the corpse she'd left behind when she was taken to the Otherworld. Life tastes very different after loss.

Mochaomhóg first began walking by the river holding his wooden beads and murmuring in that strange tongue they spoke their prayers in then. And he made sure she noticed him. It would have been hard not to; on an island full of birds, a man is strange. A threat inside the wilderness. Though Mochaomhóg would have been noticed anywhere, with his garb and peaceable smugness. I would try to move towards him sometimes, to scare him away, but it didn't work on him for some reason. Maybe there was something in the way he lived that gave him a special comfort in his skin. It made me like him even less, and my opinion had not been high initially.

He fed the birds, so they would come and sing to him and sit on his shoulders, but he didn't like animals or the natural world really. It seemed to me that what he liked was the idea of someone coming upon him, with the birds of the air and the creatures of the forest gathered round him, and marvelling at the goodness he exuded. It certainly seemed to work on Fionnuala. Months went by, and one morning he said, as he passed, 'Hello, big swan,' and she replied, 'Hello, small man,' and he pretended shock, but the conversation continued. And little by little, they became something like friends. She would sing to him, and he would listen. She would ask him questions about his new god, and he would recite various bits of gospel, and sometimes ask her questions about her life and how it had led up to this. And it could have been just what she needed. I am a hateful creature and see the threat in everyone. Maybe I am painting shadows on the memory of a nice man, out of jealousy.

I could not speak to her the way he could. Even before the curse. Certainly he made her happy for a time. She began waddling in to his hut at night and he would sleep with her two wings wrapped around him, not in a lovers' embrace, but in something more intimate, almost familial. She had a lot of sisterly affection to spare and found it hard to sleep without the warmth of her brothers beside her. And he liked to have a magical creature as his bedfellow, perhaps. He was certainly angling to convert her. Lots of talk about the benefits of his god, as opposed to the older gods who had let bad things happen to her and her family. Lots of talk about heaven, and music and welcomes and home.

He could probably have swayed me too. Fionnuala, fair play to her, took it all in her stride and was reluctant to commit to any god – kind, cruel, new or old. So eventually Mochaomhóg stopped speaking to her, saying that she was a godless creature and that he could not engage with her any further until she let him put water on her head and smear it with some oil and say some words. She held out for several months, but eventually she sighed and acquiesced. The time when her brothers were supposed to return had long since passed, and they were not with her and perhaps would never be again.

And I was there as well, but she didn't know that, and would not have welcomed it.

He was her only option for a friend.

And though she was an old, old creature, a heart still beat inside her feathered breast, and her skin still longed for comfort in the night. I know this because mine does too.

And the years passed, with her and the old hermit praying together and talking together and acting like the best of friends. And the story of the power of the holy man who had converted one of the old ones trickled through the mouths of the people who came with baskets of food for him and all along the coast until it reached somewhere it could touch danger.

And at the end of the ten years, her siblings began to return, bird by bird.

EDADH

stories   people tell

have a way   of winding

inside the   brain and

round the   heart

if you don't stop to question them

Fiachra was the first of the three to reach Inis Gluaire, and Fionnuala was both delighted and enraged to see him. Tears were shed, barbs exchanged and stories shared. Mochaomhóg took it upon himself to chide the swan for leaving his sister lonely, which endeared him further to Fionnuala, who had always been the protector and found that being protected was satisfying also. I remembered the strong arms of Dechtaire and Smól around us when we were little. Aébh on the right side, me on the left and Ailbhe, cosiest of all, in the middle. It had been so long since I had felt the touch of someone else. My heart gaped like a nestling's hungry beak.

Whatever had happened to Fiachra on his travels had left him battle-scarred. One of his eyes was grey-blue in his head and not the shining orb, dark as a void, that I was used to seeing. His voice was hoarser, as though it cost him to speak. There were raw patches on him that had not healed properly and leaked pus and dark fluid, and Mochaomhóg set about making a fine salve for these. He knew what he was at, this holy man. I wondered how he had come by that knowledge that had been sacred to my people. Had he once been a different sort of holy? It seemed to me that the new god and the old ones walked sometimes hand in hand, and it was hard to tell whose hand was whose. Both could heal, and hurt. And would, depending.

Fiachra told Fionnuala that he had been on his way back to the island, but there had been a storm, and when it cleared, he had struggled to find his path again. There had been a man waiting for him. A hard man from the north, Fiachra said, an able tracker and a decent warrior, with a thick red beard and fierce blue eyes. It had been hard enough to get away from him, he told Fionnuala, who nodded, her dark eyes glinting in the light of Mochaomhóg's cooking fire, rifling through all the different pieces of knowledge that had come to her from the mainland. She finally settled on a suspect. Lairgnen the king of Connacht. A man known for his single-mindedness and love of feats. I tended to agree.

I too had heard of this fierce king, Lairgnen, who made a sport of killing creatures no-one else could kill. The shape-shifters, the old wild boars with blood upon their tusks, and the remnants of my people too, changelings, and the old and hungry things that lived inside the lonely, rocky places. Such a man would not leave well enough alone, I knew, and the other swans would be in danger from him. I decided then to leave Fiachra and Fionnuala to their arguments and Mochaomhóg to whatever it was that he was up to, and to seek out Aodh and Conn, and see what I could do to keep them safe.

I spread my great black wings and asked the air to take me first to Aodh. They say a parent should not have a favourite, but from observing, it seems that they all do. If I ever loved them, I loved him. And when I found him, Conn was there beside him, with his twisty wing, and the two of them were together, in a thick forest, close to the Straits of Moyle. Lairgnen had indeed been tracking them, and I assumed that they had led him away from Inis Gluaire, in an effort to protect the others.

I swooped closer, between the thick, dark canopy of trees. The swans, with their wide, webbed feet, and the man were facing each other. I wondered how he'd gotten them to follow him so far out of the water. Rage perhaps. Aodh and Conn certainly seemed furious, screeching and swaying their necks to snap at him and trying to beat him with their great white wings. They were trying to kill him, and he was trying to kill them, and it seemed to me that they were both doing an equal sort of job of it. Lairgnen had beak marks on his face and his skin and clothing had been torn and mended and torn again. His sword was on the ground away from him, and he was trying to get at it. Aodh flew low to the ground towards him and hit him in the centre of his stomach. The swan and the man fell to the ground, and Conn pushed the sword deep into the undergrowth with his strong beak, before joining his brother in pecking at Lairgnen's face and neck until he ran. Aodh looked at Conn, and without words, they began to move quickly towards the water. He would be back. They had to get away.

I had always thought of Aodh and Conn as the gentler two, but in their desire to keep their family safe they were as fierce as Lir himself had been in battle. But they couldn't keep it up for ever, and it was hard to know who'd win. They were old and strong, but Lairgnen's sword or spear could do them damage. Fighting is tiring, and it only takes a very small mistake for things to go the other person's way. I resolved to do what I could to help, and being unable to hurt Lairgnen's body, I instead tried to attack his mind. The air was giving me more freedom these days, allowing me to ask for things and get them. It had taken me here without so much as a whisper of protest. I decided to push it a little further and use some of what had hurt the Children of Lir in the past to protect them in their time of need.

I visited the place where Lairgnen was sleeping, and breathed a plea to the air for a whisper of my old, dark, angry magic. It filtered through my body like a shock of cold lake water on a warm day. The moon was new, and I hovered above him, trying to mute the horror that all living creatures felt when I was near. It had abated somewhat, but what remained could be enough to thwart me. Thankfully, the air was kind to me, and cruel to him. I felt a push, and then I was in his dreams and weaving them to my will. I sent him opened throats and leather bindings. I sent him death beneath the watery earth, sunk deep inside the bog but living still, and watching as he turned from man to a leathery, preserved thing. I sent him beaks that nibbled at the soft meat of his cheeks, exposing jaw. I sent him a year inside a dark room, with a man who will not love you or leave you be. I sent him the face of the hound of Ulster in a battle frenzy, and the teeth of him tearing and pulling at the skin of his enemies. I sent him a poisoned weapon through the stomach, and the barbs of it digging in and sending venom all around his body so he would die screaming in his own filth. I sent him how I saw him, how small he was and how much I would do to him, and maybe could, if the cruel air would let me. I sent him how old the swans were, how much they had suffered, and how much more than he had it would take to break them.

And the dark magic that I poured into his brain was a poison well made. He tried repeatedly to wake but I held fast to him, binding him to me like we were lovers. And when he woke, he had lost a portion of himself and ran. Not home, to his kingdom, but just away, from what his mind became. Away to bind the pieces of himself that I had shattered back together into something resembling the man that he had been. And you shall see, as I saw, how that worked for him.

And what a joy it was to use my skills again! To feel that power rushing through me. I had felt guilt for doing what I had to my sister's children, but there was not a drop of guilt for what I did to Lairgnen. Perhaps that is how warriors feel when they kill in battle. I do not know. Perhaps by then, people just seemed so ... short-lived. Little may-fly things that stormed and stamped and mated and moved on and lived and died all in the space of a heartbeat.

I did stop short of destroying him altogether, which may have been foolhardy. But I just needed him broken enough to forget what he was at and give the two some time to find Fionnuala. I had a sense that a lot of her strength was in how her brothers saw her and that Mochaomhóg wouldn't be long falling in line when her confidence was back.

Conn and Aodh, as Fiachra said he had done, spent time making their way back, weaving this way and that way to avoid pursuit. They needn't have bothered, but there was no way to tell them that, exhausted as I was. There was nothing left of me. The air gave me the shape of a cormorant soon after I had done what I did to Lairgnen, and I forgot most of who I was for a sweet and salty stretch of time.

SCÉAL

Mochaomhóg made a fine silver chain for the swans, and they walked around him, in perfect trust, and the distress and discomfort that had been their lot was just a memory. And they sang their beautiful songs at holy mass, and so the fame of the Children of Lir spread across the land once more, and Deoch, the daughter of the king of Munster, heard tell of them and could not be happy until they were in her possession, so she called on her husband, Lairgnen of Connacht, to procure the swans for her by whatever means he could. And Lairgnen sent messengers to ask Mochaomhóg to part with the swans, but the holy man would not. So Lairgnen set out towards the island, and he thinking of her goading him on all the while.

When I returned to the four swans and their new best friend, the scheming hermit, the way things were was different. Fionnuala, buoyed up by the return of her brothers, did not pressure them to renounce their godless ways, pointing out to Mochaomhóg that they already had renounced their gods and didn't care for new ones. Nor did she. She didn't need the holy man's company in the same way that she had, and her sureness of herself had returned. She hadn't been abandoned. There had been a threat. And there was still a threat. But she had weathered terrible things with her family beside her.

She had gathered information about Lairgnen, and I was impressed by her cunning. It was easy for me to spy on people – they couldn't see me, and I could hear many things all at once. But she was a massive swan who stayed in one place, mainly. And yet, she had managed to piece together as much as I, and more.

What they knew of him tallied with what I did, and built upon where I had left him, terrified. When I am in the body of a bird, I do not fear the future in the same way that I did when I was human. The sense of self I left inside the swans was a curse as well as a kindness. But I do not know if I could have taken it away, with words and wand, who they had been and would be, who they were. I have tried for a long time to escape who I am, and the things I am capable of when I feel trapped or backed into a corner. The anger that feeds me burns me too, and leaves scars in its wake that I can trace thousands of years later. And even when I lose the sense of who I am, when what magic remains within me leaches out of me, fragments of the whole will still be there and seek to fit the one to the other. And I know that I will still find something to enrage me. The closest thing, perhaps. Myself. My self. You can't run from your shadow: the light will bend and it will always find you.

Lairgnen's breakdown didn't stop him being who he was. He was the sort of person who would take what he wanted from the world and survive that way. And he continued to do so, forcing his way through the wilderness until it gave, and he found people who would nurse him back to health, in the kingdom of Finghin, son of Aodh Allain. Finghin had a daughter called Deoch. And Lairgnen wanted her, and because he was the son of a king, and a fine figure of a man besides, he was used to getting the things that he wanted. Politically, it was an excellent match, but it is hard to know what Deoch might have wanted, who she was. Almost a thousand years after I had been a girl who had married a powerful man, she was a girl who married a powerful man. We were both selfish creatures in the one story, and that forges a bond of sorts, I think. But I wondered how she felt about the whole endeavour. She certainly seemed keen to make it difficult for him to get her. And whether that was in service to holding his interest or holding him at bay, I cannot really know. It is enough to tell you that I wondered.

Deoch and Lairgnen were wed, and soon after she began demanding that he go to Inis Gluaire and procure for her the swans. Knowing that he had come close to death the last time he had dallied with them, she asked this of him. Perhaps she just liked swans. Or having things that other people didn't. Perhaps she could see that Lairgnen was set upon going to them anyway, the rarity of the defeat nagging and pinching at him as he went about his day, and even more sharply when the day was done and he lay beside his wife, their breaths mingling in the air and the night pooling dark around them, black as the inky eyes of a feathered adversary.

The story, at any rate, is that she was spoilt and demanding, and felt a powerful urge to have those swans, with all their songs and stories, for her own. She wanted to put gold collars around their necks and affix chains to those collars that all went into one thick gold chain that she would have in her hands, and so pull them around. A leash, people would call it now. Something that tethers what is yours to you and prevents it from going where it will. There are some who claim Mochaomhóg kept a chain around the swans' necks, but he wouldn't have been long for this world if he'd chanced it, friend or foe. They had been tethered to place after place, and to each other, for such a long time. He did take care of them, and that bound them to him in a kinder way, the same way that I was bound to the people I had loved, well and ill, when I was in a body that could touch them.

Lairgnen sent messengers to the island, where the Four were waiting, with their holy man, who would be predictably useless in any sort of altercation. And the messengers asked for the swans, and were refused by the swans, and then by the holy man. And the supposed power of Mochaomhóg's new god was enough to put the fear into the messengers, and they did not unsheathe their swords and bloody the earth around them, but rather made their way back to report what had gone on to Lairgnen, who had been waiting for their refusal so he could move with force.

SCÉAL

Lairgnen arrived at the island and stormed into the chapel with a great anger upon him. He seized the holy man and demanded to know if it was true that he had refused him the thing that he had asked for, and the hermit said that it was, and the young king was seized by a great anger, and he did seize two of the swans by their necks with one hand, and then wrapped his other hand around the other two, and set off down to bring them home to Deoch. But no sooner had he touched the swans than they transformed once more into human form, leaving three ancient men and a crone lying atop piles of soft white feathers. And Lairgnen was taken aback, and he left the holy man to tend to the Children of Lir and returned to his fort much unsettled.

EAMHANCOLL

whatever lies beyond this world of ours I am not fool enough to think I know it

no boats

but

and

I do know what I wish for those

to take

ears

hearts

I've loved; an island of their own

them

that

that

where they can take whatever shape

no words

hear

hold

they want and still be welcome

to hurt them

them

them

They moved to the chapel when they sensed him arriving. Flapping their wings, and snapping their beaks, the swans were ready for a fight, and I was there to try my best to help them. The hermit wanted peace. He was afraid, I think, of what the consequences would be, for his way of life, if he was party to the killing of a king. And the swans would have killed Lairgnen, I think, in their wilder days, on the Straits of Moyle, when they felt abandoned by all belonging to them and raged under the weight of what I'd done. Mochaomhóg bid them stop, and his lips murmured, praying for them to calm, and it worked like a spell and perhaps it was a sort of spell. Perhaps there was something to the new god, I remember thinking. Whether this power came from the same source with a different name or was a new thing entirely, it stilled them.

Fionnuala folded her wings into two soft curves with a valley between them, and her brothers did the same. They eyed the hermit, and Aodh made a low croaking in his throat, not an angry noise, but the noise of a great white bird and not an old, old child who had been hurt and hurt and hurt again by the people who were meant to love him.

The old man urged them to come with him inside the chapel, as Lairgnen was less likely to desecrate the house of god than a place that only belonged to nature. And I looked at the green grass turning crisp, and the grey stones of the island, and the rushes, and I thought of the sacred spaces I had known back in Sídh Femuin, where I had been a girl with my sisters. I remembered the peace of my two feet at the ground and the tall trees all around me and the golden sunlight filtering through them like a blessing, like a promise, and why, when all of that was all around you, would you need four walls to find your god?

The air cut a thin, sharp line from my head between my wings, right down the centre of me, as though it were trying to slice me in two, to warn me of something. I don't know what it wanted, but I pushed against its will. I had a sick, strange feeling in my stomach, a sense of ... well, it's hard to know what it was a sense of. Dread and I were always hand in hand, and so much time has passed since the day I'm telling you about that, when I colour it in, I am telling you from the future what seems to be the present. I know what will happen to this man, to these swans. To the king, and to Deoch, as well. I have been all of them, one way or another as I turned it over and over in my brain, long after the parts of the story people care about have ended.

I have been a sister who cared for her siblings, who tried to keep them safe. I have been protected, I have been fierce, I have been strange. I have been alone and close to higher powers, I have been angry at the world and fought to master those around me, I have been a king's unhappy wife. No-one blameless, no-one without cause. People are not born exactly how they are; life shapes them, like hands on clay can form a spoon, a bowl, a chalice or a lantern. I was everyone inside that chapel and I followed them, and they knew that I did. I could tell from the stiffening of their long white necks. The poise with which they held their soft white bodies. The deliberate movement of their flapping feet that slapped the one after the other along the earth and then across the stone. When they reached the threshold, I waited by the door to see when he would come and if there was something that I could do to stop him taking them across the water to his dwelling place, to live away from the home they had long-sought and found too late.

The boat moving across the water and the stretch of it widening, widening, yawning between three little girls and a life that could have been, if not better, different perhaps. My hand on Aébh's belly and the dance of the twins inside, the strangeness and the miracle of that. And what I'd done. I breathed the air inside me in my lungs and felt the mist inside it and the earth that water had come from and would return to. My breath was sharp and I worked hard to slow it, but the fire was in my throat and I wished that I could speak, that they could hear me. I wished that I could tell them how sorry I was and how I had tried, and how I would try, to keep them safe. But those words would only have been for myself to hear. They needed my help, and not a vow or an apology or something soft and useless made of words.

I heard the harsh tramp of feet approach the chapel, across muck and rush and rock and grass and pool until they met the flag. And he was as tall and strong-looking as he had been the last time that I saw him. And the same fire in my throat was in his eyes and they were intent on that chapel. And I spread my two big wings and stood in front of it and he stopped still at the door and looked at the four swans and the old man standing together, by the altar. Staring at him with their ten bright eyes. Human and inhuman. And he stared back. He tried to push through me. And it felt dreadful, like my flesh were a bowl of porridge and he a hungry mouse who'd fallen in, scrabbling desperately at the meat of me, pushing it this way and that as he tried his best to cling to life. Aodh's voice rang through the chapel:

'Let him enter.'

And I, agog, did just what I was told. Lairgnen shook himself like a dog, and looked around with the frightened eyes of the young man he was, before swallowing and deciding to follow through on the reason that he had come. Mochaomhóg stood behind the swans, his lips shaping the new god's words, over and over again. I would have had more respect for him, I think, if he had tried harder to protect them, but cowardice is often something that can't be controlled.

My sister Ailbhe, had she been there, would have stared Lairgnen down and sent him packing. Or sliced his head from his neck. I longed for her, knowing that wherever she had gone, she was now dead. The Four were the closest thing I had to family. I tried to inch my way inside the chapel. It was difficult. There was a strong sense that this place, whatever holiness it had, was not for me, or people who were like me. However, I was used to feeling unwelcome, to pushing at the limits of what Bodhbh had done to me and forcing myself against them until I felt them give. I eased my way inside, and it was a dim but warm little place. There was not that much space to it. Lairgnen could have taken three small steps and stood beside the swans and yet he stood, feet planted on the ground, and stared at the little monk, the holy man.

'Give them to me,' he demanded of the holy man.

And Fionnuala rose on her thick stone-coloured feet to her full height. Larger and more imposing than a normal swan, she was as tall as Mochaomhóg but a head shorter than Lairgnen. Aodh, Conn and Fiachra rose up as well and held their wings out, daring him to come closer. I wormed my way between him and them and held my wings out too, making as large an invisible barrier as I could.

'We are not his to give,' Fionnuala told him.

And Lairgnen took a step closer. I could feel his hot breath on and in me, moving through the air in the small space. He drew his sword and reached out a hand. If I could be a crow to peck his eyes out, an owl to claw his scalp to bloody shreds. If I could find a way to help the children of Aébh, I thought. And I prayed to the air to let me stop this man. To let them have the hard-won peace that they deserved. He unsheathed his sword and reached a meaty hand out to grab at them. By luck, or by design, I'm not sure which, his fist clamped around Fiachra's neck. Aodh's sharp beak went for the fist itself, and Conn went for those piercing blue eyes that were so intent on having something that should not be had, on owning something that should not be owned.

'Leave us be,' the Four said, facing him down, but he did not, and his hand squeezed around Fiachra's throat, though one of his eyes was bleeding. So they tore and pecked at him until he had to let go. Not seeking to injure him, or only as much as was necessary to protect themselves. And perhaps it could have ended differently, but Lairgnen was a king who had been crossed, and he began wildly swinging his sword around, hacking and screaming, until all I could see was a cloud of blood and feathers, and I tried to reach through it and pull his weapon from his hand, or give him wild, cold thoughts to send him reeling. But I couldn't help. All I could do was watch, as the monk crouched away behind the altar, peeping out every now and then. The helplessness he felt mirrored what was in my heart, and I felt a strange kinship with him.

After a time, it slowed down, and the swans parted, leaving the king upon the altar, bruised and blood-soaked. They had not emerged unscathed, and I could see their own red blood had mingled with Lairgnen's. A stain at Fionnuala's breast, as red and pulsing as a heart, looked mortal. One of Aodh's eyes was gone, and Fiachra gasped as though the air were knives. Conn was covered in small gashes, and it was hard to know who to tend to first.

Mochaomhóg ran to Lairgnen, and checked that he was breathing, and I followed the swans out into the cold air of Inis Gluaire, and towards the ending of their tale, and some of mine.

And a pale and uncertain light was hanging over the island that morning, with the palest golden strands hanging like the hair of Lugh, but an older Lugh, where the gold is filtered through with silver-grey. So much time had passed, I thought, since the gods walked the earth among us, and magic was there for the reaching of a hand and the wanting of a heart.

But I felt the flow of it again, and something else. The mist began to glow and pool, and it descended upon us, and I felt my two feet touch the ground, not the feet of a bird, or the claws of the demon I'd become, but my own two feet that I had had before. And I felt the power of the earth flowing into me again, and something older and wiser than I would ever be drawing closer and closer, until I couldn't think, but only feel.

SCÉAL

And Fionnuala did say to Mochaomhóg, 'Come and baptise us now, for death is fast approaching.' And her next instruction was to bury them as they had slept in life, with Fionnuala in the middle, giving shelter, with Conn on the left and Fiachra on her right, and her own twin Aodh before her.

And the holy man did all that she had asked of him, and put a stone over their grave, and their names were written on it in the Ogham. And Mochaomhóg spent time at the stone, weeping and being sorrowful after them, though he knew their suffering was at an end, and their souls were safe in heaven.

And so ends the fate of the Children of Lir.

Here I was.

I looked down at my hands. I touched my hair. And then what had just happened came rushing back to me and I groped wildly through the mist to find them, until my hands touched, not blood and feathers, but soft grey hair and tender skin. The air cleared and I could see four shapes beside me, four old people, with long white hair and ink-dark eyes. They looked at me.

How could they look at me?

It wasn't possible. I thought. *And yet …*

'Aífe,' said the woman, and it was the rasping voice of Fionnuala. 'We don't have long, you need to get Mochaomhóg.'

So I ran back the short distance to the chapel, and pulled the hermit from the wounded king, and dragged him with me. His face was pale, and there were questions that he almost asked. I could sense them rising up and dipping away. The lump inside his throat was bobbing, and when he saw the four long bodies curled around each other, his face grew pale, and he began to pray again.

'There is no time for that, my friend,' Fionnuala told him. And he knew who she was and held her hand and looked at her with complicated love. She blinked at him.

'You need to tell your god to let me go.'

'I can't,' he gasped. 'You cannot ask me that.'

'I can and I will,' she said. 'We're going to die, and soon. And in the Otherworld, I want to be with them, beside my brothers, like I was in life. And if I'm not, if I am somewhere else, I will be lonely and they will be lonely. We have been through so much. Mochaomhóg, please.'

And he nodded, and began to recite words in that same strange tongue he said his prayers in, but these words were harsher and felt older. I could feel a ripple through the earth as though it were reaching out to hold the swans, to claim them back again.

Fionnuala's head relaxed and her body settled down upon the earth. She squeezed the old man's hand and gave him thanks. He moved away from them, in fear or awe, I'm not sure which. I felt a mixture of both as well. They drew together, as close as they had been when they were curled together from the storm, but their expressions were not angry or stoic or fearful. There was a sort of radiance to them. A calm. And I felt so ashamed of what I'd done. Looking at them, knowing that the end of it was coming, and that they would move away, I tried to speak, but whatever spell was on me wouldn't let me and the words caught in my throat and tears came to my eyes.

And Aodh said, 'Aífe.'

And they all turned, and I felt their eyes on me and I felt as hideous as all my cruelty, and it was as though no time at all had passed and they were four little children, looking at me, and I was ruining them again, again. I backed away.

'Aífe.'

I wasn't sure whose voice it was, one of them, but my thoughts were clouded with self-loathing.

'Come.'

And I looked at my feet and urged them to obey, and step by step I moved to be beside the children of my sister.

'Will you say the words, and bury us when we are dead?'

I couldn't speak. I wanted so to speak. But I just nodded.

Fionnuala turned to me. 'That is good. We will go to the Otherworld soon. And we will tell our mother what you have done to us, but also what you have done for us. And she will forgive you, Aífe, as we have.'

And the ground went from under me. And I collapsed, and the mist came down upon the Four, and when it rose again, it had taken their spirits with them. And I was there alone and back inside the form I knew the best. My demon's body.

I looked down at my strong wings and sharp talons. I could not see my eyes, but if I squinted I could get a shadow of the grey of my beak. I scooped them up in my two great wings, as though they weighed nothing at all. And I washed their bodies and made offerings and said the words and buried them the way my people were buried. And I placed Fionnuala at the centre, Aodh before her, Fiachra on her right and Conn on her left. The way they had liked best to be in life. And I felt myself fade away from the world again and turn into the sort of thing I had been for a thousand years and more, the sort of thing that cannot touch the world. At least not in the way that others can.

But I was there, as the holy man tended to the wounded king and sent him on his way with a story that they both agreed to tell, where souls and dignity could both be saved. I was there as he placed a cross over their burial ground and said his prayers, while knowing in his heart that his new god could not contain the old heart of a wild thing.

That there were miracles that were not his.

I was there, looking and remembering, as feet tramped towards the grave and looked, as their story was changed and changed again, and told and sung and written down in manuscripts and books. As pictures were drawn of them, and in each they took a slightly different shape, and a part of the truth but not the truth entirely.

No more than this story, which is mine, but more than mine, and which my memories have no doubt sculpted into something just a little different from what happened.

And there I was.

A thousand years and more have passed since then.

And here I am.

Though I would like to die, I'll never die.

And someone will always remember the children of Aébh and what was done to them. And how they survived and found a place that was their own.

And lived together, and then died together.

And how, against all odds, they could forgive.

Aífe

Fionnuala

Fiachra   Conn

Aodh

Our people came in a mist, and the children of Aébh departed in one. I do not know where people go. And I will never know. But I can hope. They gave that back to me.

And I hope for them that they are in the Otherworld, where you can live a whole new life again, in a place of welcome. Where suffering is eased, and the things our people loved – fighting, feasts, the building blocks of story – are always sliding into place around you. And I hope that in the next world they built their own story and that it was smaller and kinder than a legend or a fairytale. I hope that Conn got to have a family, and Fionnuala a kingdom to rule, Fiachra a gang of warriors to join, and Aodh, my sweet Aodh … Maybe he will have written down his version of the story I have told you. And perhaps it will be different to mine, as night is to day, though they take place in a cycle. We are all journeying through the same place. The air is thinner now in places, and thick with dirt in others, as unlike the air I lived in once as sugar water is to thick dark honey. My people have died off, little by little, or the gateways between our world and the world of humans have shut tightly. Which is a shame for me, but in many ways a piece of luck for the people who live on the island now.

And I live many lives. I am a cormorant, a corncrake. I am a blackbird, a raven, though I have no taste for pain, having seen enough. I am a starling, sometimes, or a swallow. I flit between the shapes and I taste the air with very different lungs. I nest, I fly. I cannot touch the other lives around me, but I can look at them and I can love.

I never found out what became of Ailbhe. But sometimes, as I listened to stories shared, while I hid my little form outside a door, on a windowsill or in the thatch, and later on, on balconies, or on the canopy over a piece of garden, near friends on walks who stop and share old half-remembered tales from when they were small, I gathered little snatches. There was a woman warrior who trained with Scathach, as I had counselled her to do, and they were lovers or, in some tales, sisters, for a time, and then they quarrelled and she assembled her own band of warriors. She bore a son who died at his father's hands. And the heartbreak claimed her. But she lived long before that. And drank deep of life. And was feared and was loved and was present in the world. They spoke of her skill in battle and her long red hair. An Irish woman warrior in Alban.

Her name was Aífe.

And so my sister may have kept me with her, my name at least, though Bodhbh's hold on me would not allow us to see each other again, in life or death. No-one can contain the human heart, and hers always beat more fiercely than mine. That urge to fight in some people is like a boil to drain. In her, it stemmed, I think, more from a desire to protect. To ensure our safety and her own. That we might never again be frightened and alone, not knowing who we were and what it meant. And I cannot be sure if this story of another Aífe and the sister that I knew are one and the same. And maybe they are not. But my Ailbhe would not have lived life quietly. And she was generous and loved me. It's not impossible.

It is also possible that Bodhbh's soldiers found and slaughtered her, but this is my story, mine, and even after all this time, I hope. I have been given that.

For things can change.

Children turn to swans, they suffer and they suffer, they forgive you. My enemy the air becomes my home. The world turns around and teems with life, with people. Creatures live and die and live again, well and badly, happily and unhappily. People transform into other people and find ways to build homes inside their pain. To find a refuge. Miracles occur. There is no understanding on the heart.

But round and round we go.

There is no ending.

I come from   this world

I came from a world where people do terrible things to each other all the time

I am a woman I am a demon I am a witch I am a bird I am the air I am a story half-told I am a liar I am a shrew I am a wife I am a daughter I am abandoned I am together I am a sister I am alone I am a harpy I am transformed I am a shadow I am a light I am a force I am a curse I am invisible I am a shiver I am a pulse I am your gooseflesh I am a watcher I am a helper I am a teller I am a fixer I am a criminal I am sentenced I am punished I am trying I am failing I am trying I am keeping I am reaching I am listening I am learning I am hearing I am trying I am hurting I am wanting I am loving I am watching I am staying I am staying I am living I am breathing I am feeling I am needing I am silent I am speaking I am telling I am thinking I am sharing I am lonely I am strong I am refuge I am terror I am foolish I am ancient I am knowing I am learning I am leaning I am loving I am waiting I am hoping I am fearing I am hurting I am trying I am here I am here I am here I am here I am a crow I am a gull I am a crow I am a sparrow I am a wren I am a corncrake I am a robin I am a bird I am feathered I am leathered I am old I am young I am a crone I am a girl I am a storm I am a bird I am a witch I am a woman I am a demon I am alive.

NAMES

Pronunciations shown in brackets are approximate only.
Characters who appear once or twice only are not listed.

Aífe (Efa): the narrator
Aébh (Ave): Aífe's elder sister
Ailbhe (Alva): Aífe's younger sister
Oillill (Al-ill) of Aran and Éabha (Ay-va): parents of Aífe and her sisters
Bodhbh Dearg (Bov Jarg), Bodhbh the Red or simply Bodhbh (Bov):
  their foster-father and high king of Ireland
Dechtaire (Dec-tharra) and Smól (Smole): female warriors, who look
  after Aífe and her sisters when young

Lir: a chieftain,
Aodh (Ae, rhymes with hay): son of Aébh and Lir, twin of Fionnuala
Fionnuala (Finnu-uh-la): daughter of Aébh and Lir, twin of Aodh
Fiachra (Fee-acra): son of Aébh and Lir, twin of Conn
Conn (as spelt): son of Aébh and Lir, twin of Fiachra

Mochaomhóg (Muh-kweevoh-g): a monk or holy man
Lairgnen (Larg-nen): king of Connacht
Deoch (Juk): wife of Lairgnen
Finghin (Finnian): a king, father of Deoch

(The) Dagda (as spelt): chief god
Danu (Dan-u or Dana): chief goddess
Tuatha Dé Danann (Thoo-ha day Dannan): the people of the goddess
  Danu
Manannán Mac Lir (Manan-awn Mac Lir): a sea god
Lugh Lámhfhada (Lou Lawv-adda): Lugh of the Long Arm, a god
Oisín (Usheen): a warrior

Niamh (Neave): a princess, wife of Oisín
Fianna (Fee-unna): a powerful army of warriors

(The) Morrigan (as spelt): goddess of war, a shape-changer
Aengus Óg (Aeng-gus Owg): a god, a shape-changer
Caer (Care): his lover, a water sprite
Scathach (Ska-huck): a Scottish warrior woman and trainer of warriors

Etain (Aideen): a princess
Midir (as spelt): her lover
Fuamnach (Foov-nyck): his wife

PLACE NAMES

Alban (as spelt): Scotland
Aran (as spelt): an archipelago consisting of three islands
Carraig na Rón (Carrick na Rone): the rock of the seals
Éirinn (Ai-rin): a grammatical form of Éire, Ireland
Inis Gluaire (Inish Glora): an island
Iorrus Domnann (Irris Duvnan): Erris, a place in the West of Ireland
Loch Dairbhreach (Lock Dav-rock): Lake Derravaragh
Sídh Finnachadh (Shee Finn-uh-kuh): home of Lir
Sídh Femuin (Shee Fev-in): home of Bodhbh

OTHER WORDS

ficheall (feak-ill): a game like chess
Ogham (Owe-am or ogg-am): an ancient script; note that the chapter
    headings represent letters of the Ogham alphabet
scéal (shkale): a story
sídh (shee): a magical dwelling place

A NOTE ON THE USE OF OGHAM

Between the chapters of this book you will have seen calligrams, poems laid out in particular shapes. Those shapes mimic the characters, or letters, of the earliest Irish alphabet, which is called Ogham. The characters of Ogham came to be associated with particular words, and many are linked to trees. There is a power and a poetry to the words and phrases associated with each letter, and I found myself returning to it, looking at it, and wondering how I could connect it to Aífe, who is so hungry for knowledge and for love.

Poetry and the importance of the poet weaves its way through Irish myth and culture. Poetry can be a way to speak unspoken things. I thought a lot about retelling and reclaiming when writing *Savage Her Reply*, of taking something old and making it new. The poems reflect that.

I'm not an historian or an expert, and if you would like to find out more about Ogham, some sources that helped me as I researched *Savage Her Reply* include work by old Irish experts Damian McManus and Catherine Swift, and popular writers such as Lora O'Brien and James MacKillop.

ACKNOWLEDGEMENTS

Books don't just happen. *Savage Her Reply* can be traced back to my
childhood, where the librarians in Galway City Library supported and
indulged my love of books. That's where I first encountered Michael
Scott's retelling of The Children of Lir, the book that connected me to
Aífe's story. I'm so grateful to librarians for the work they do, and the
worlds they open up.

I'd like to thank my agent Clare Wallace for her warm and tireless
support, Sheila David for her kindness and Mary Darby, Georgia Fuller,
Kristina Egan, Rosanna Bellingham, Lydia Silver and Chloe Davis at
Darley Anderson for the work they've done to help my books along.

This book wouldn't have happened without the faith that Little Island
Books have in me. Siobhán Parkinson, mentor, editor, champion and
friend, I am so grateful to work with you. I hope you like your book.
To Matthew Parkinson-Bennett, thank you for the time, care and
enthusiasm you put into *Savage Her Reply*. I really appreciate it. Gráinne
Clear, who was there at the very first meeting about the book, Kate
McNamara, Elizabeth Goldrick and Aurélie Connan for their helpful
insights along the way, and Nina Douglas for wonder and witchcraft.

If you've read this book, you can probably sense that it wasn't an easy book to write, and while I was working on it the support of other writers meant so much. Mark Ward, Sarah Maria Griffin, Dave Rudden, Sarah Davis Goff, Claire Hennessy and Ciara Banks (my first publisher) offered support in different ways over the journey of making this, and I'm very appreciative.

I am also thankful for the deep knowledge and kind heart of the wonderful Dr Kelly Fitzgerald. While *Savage Her Reply* is a work of fiction, it is grounded in a deep wealth of myth and folklore. The insight of someone who lives and breathes these stories was a true privilege. I'm also deeply grateful to Richard Marsh for kindly pointing me in the right direction while I was researching, and to Teresa Coyne for taking the time to recommend some books. There is something really special about people who are generous with their wisdom, and I'm very grateful to all of you.

While researching this book, work by Jefrey Kantz, James MacKillop, Eithne Massey, Miranda J Green, Paul Sterry, Will Worthington, John Matthews, Jack Roberts, Michael Scott, Thomas Campbell, Morgan Llywelyn, Ann Dooley and Harry Roe, Marie Louise Sjoestedt, Eileen O'Faoláin, Eugene O'Curry, Augusta Gregory, Marie Heaney, Peter Berresford Ellis and Richard Marsh was particularly helpful.

To Karen Vaughan, it's such a privilege to be working with you again.

To booksellers, getting books to the people that need them, in good times and strange ones. Thank you for your support, care and dedication to what you do.

To Children's Books Ireland for kindly granting me the time and space to work on this project with a bursary to the Tyrone Guthrie Centre. Your support for this and my other books has been such a gift.

To anyone who has taken the time to read and review my work, to post about it or press it into the hands of a friend. It means the world.

To Mom, Dad, Tadhg and Cameron, Carmel, John L, Nana, Jerry, Mary, Josie, May and Donnacha. I'm glad we're family.

To my Diarmuid, on old roads and on new ones.
Grá mo chroí thú.

ABOUT THE AUTHOR

Deirdre Sullivan is an award-winning writer from Galway in the West of Ireland. *Savage Her Reply* is her tenth book. Her collection of dark and witchy fairytale retellings, *Tangleweed and Brine* (Little Island Books), won Book of the Year at the 2018 Children's Books Ireland awards and Young Adult Book of the Year at the 2017 Irish Book Awards.

Other books for young adults include *Perfectly Preventable Deaths* (Hot Key, 2019) and, with Little Island Books, *Needlework* (Honour Award for Fiction, Children's Books Ireland awards 2017), the Primrose Leary trilogy (*Prim Improper, Improper Order* and *Primperfect* – the first YA book to be shortlisted for the EU Prize for Literature in 2015). For younger readers, she has written three books in the Nightmare Club series.

Deirdre also writes short fiction and poetry, which has been published in places like *Banshee, The Penny Dreadful, Mslexia* and the *Dublin Review*. Her play *Wake* was performed by No Ropes theatre company in February 2019.

ABOUT LITTLE ISLAND BOOKS

Little Island Books publishes good books for young minds, from toddlers to older teens. Little Island specialises in new Irish writers and illustrators, and also has a commitment to publishing books in translation. Little Island was founded in 2010 and *Savage Her Reply* is Little Island's 100th book.

www.littleisland.ie